Blue Eyed Raven

Blue Eyed Raven

Sam Raven

To order additional copies of this book, contact:
Xlibris
844-714-8691
www.Xlibris.com
Orders@Xlibris.com
833951

Chapter 1

Sam sat with his eyes looking down thinking how long it had been since he was here. His mind flashed back many years, thinking of the times when he would meet Jack back in the woods past Cracker Swamp and just outside of Roy, but a piece between the Quarters and potato farms in Hastings where swamps were thick and the fox ran free.

Uncle Jack had hounds that were true-blooded and had registered names, the kind dogs that in a trial would be awarded the best in show! Sam, who tried to imitate city folk, was just unable to be like them. And in turn, he wasn't generally accepted by the white people. He was there but never felt the same.

While others lived for what they could become, Sam thanked every day for sunshine, rain, animals, and nature's living things. As a child alone, he would think of things to play with. His mother said he was a dreamer with big ideas. Maybe someday he might succeed and turn away to go back to work. She would wash, cook, and work to have money enough to give his sister so they could be like the rest.

They lived in a poor section outside of town in the countryside on the Desilburger Estate. As a child, Sam would run and play in swamps woods, fish in the creeks, rivers, lakes, and ponds. He would keep his dogs free so they would go where they pleased. Everyone knew the names of the dogs and the owner. When they came to eat your dog's food, you just ran them back home so there wouldn't be a fight, or you'd just let the dogs settle it between each other.

This night was special for Sam, one that came along just in time to help keep Sam sane. In the Army, he would do things that the other men would not or could not do. Maybe it was the Power that was given to him by unseen hands, that Unknown Spirit worshiped by the white man but lived with Indian of the land, Spirit of the past that lingers and guides to show a way through troubles of the day, the power that's always there to raise you high above the danger that is instilled by want and greed, the power that makes you unseen to evil or the angel of death during war. Finding peace with his hounds who share his soul to run free at night, chasing the ever so cunning fox that, like a slippery ghost, runs to play, then in an instant, disappears leaving tired hounds to run again another night. The mind skitters along in space from place to place trying not to linger too long, afraid that you might lose your place knowing that it happened, but you're still alive crouched here on a knee reading signs and waiting for the fox to announce that he has jumped and the race is on.

Back at the truck, there is fat lighter for a fire. After the alpha hound Red jumps, the other hounds will join in. That's when we will settle down and wait just listen to the *music* the hounds make. Sam can tell which dog is out front.

This night, the air is cold ... the kind of cold that is so biting it feels like a razor cutting through your skin. After building a fire, Sam tries to dodge the acrid smell coming in black smoke circles which dance upward into the darkness. The smoke clings to your clothes with a stench that lingers until you wash them, a scent that tells you that you have been close to fire.

In the distance, Sam hears the sound of an owl calling out. The fire crackles and pops with energy alive to consume the resin of pine seeping from seams in the fat lighter wood which splits open due to the dry heat of the flames.

In ditches alongside the road, overflow of water used to flood potato fields stands silent encased with a cover of ice.

Taking a stick, Sam walks down the road away from the sounds close to the truck so he can listen to the hounds. Reaching down with the stick, he taps on the ice in the ditch breaking it like glass while thinking about the dogs feet as they run through this same frozen water. Dogs have turned, coming back towards the road, and Sam thinks maybe the fox will cross and the hounds will be close behind. This is a smart fox that has been running for a while. This should be a good 6- or 8-hour race. Darn good thing Sam thinks to bring his gloves, since the tips of his fingers feel numb, "like my feet," he thinks. Walking around causes his feet to burn, so Sam stamps the ground while rubbing his hands together, moving back towards the fire.

The hounds are close now. Picking up the light, he moves toward the spot where he thinks the fox might cross. Just off to the side, he hears sounds. The fox is running parallel to the road, so he clicks on the light. No sign of the fox, but here come the hounds.

Red's in the lead with Judy number three. All of the young dogs are in between. Mr. Fox runs down the side of the road another 45 or 50 feet, then he crosses, making a loop, then he heads for the swamp.

Walking back to the fire, Sam thinks to himself about the pleasure he gets from being alone in nature with his hounds. There's "*no need to*" or "*got to be done*" until after the race when he gathers up all the dogs to go back home.

The sun is starting to break just as the hounds start coming in with tired steam coming off of their coats. As the gate to the dog box is opened, Sam gently helps each one load up. The loaded dogs lay down tired, waiting for the others to come in. After the last one has been loaded up, this is when Sam could really use a hot cup of coffee.

Coming out of Cracker Swamp Road, the houses Sam passes haven't even started to get up yet. "It's too early," he thinks. Taking the old road home, he goes by the truck stop at Pellicer Creek, and a quick stop there will give Sam time enough to get some coffee, then make it home at a decent hour.

Inside the truck, the heater sure does feel good on Sam's feet. Pulling into the parking lot of the truck stop, he parks beside a pick-up that belongs to an ole boy who lives nearby the hounds, the hounds.

Alike in most ways, it was Sam the dog man, and Suz the Bird Woman! Here at home in this small fishing village, the Spirits held onto each other's aura causing a wall to be erected between the two.

Later on after Sam got his coffee and was headed home, he thought about Suz, the bird woman. She was light into his lonely life and, oh, how that woman could love. Living in her own world, Suz allowed no one in. Sam had heard her say *"If you take me, you must take all of me."* She was most like Sam, caring for nature's animals and forest. She loved to be free to fly with the birds, as much as he loved a run with Sam's mother, a Spirit, held this power and spell, not allowing him to find happiness with a woman that he loved. Instead he took time to find kindness and understanding in the wild.

Each morning, Sam went outside to check on the home he had built for birds and squirrels. He checked on the dogs, flowers, fruit, and food stuff that were planted for wild animals to eat.

Sam's home was in a natural hammock-like sanctuary where wild animals passing through felt at home and got a meal before traveling on.

Spirit Woman, Bird Woman's mother, had trying times before her mortal frame left and her spirit flew into life's cloudy sky. Bird Woman is daughter of Spirit Woman, whose other daughter teaches and lives on Black Water Bayou, deep in the swamps, in Cajun land.

Sam pulls into the yard, backs up to the dog pen so the dogs can be unloaded after a night's run. Sam slams the truck's door and walks to the back talking along the way to the hounds which are still in the dog box. He goes into the hound's pen and gives them fresh water. Walking back to the truck, Sam opens the dog box door and all the dogs try to come out at the same time. Sam grabs a collar in each hand and pulls, placing Red and Judy into the pen so the others will follow. Closing the door after the last pup was inside, Sam moves toward the back door of the house thinking about a hot shower and taking a nap, maybe getting a bite to eat.

Later in the afternoon, he would slip down into the lower pasture to check on the cows and horses, putting out mineral and flakes of hay before coming up and feeding the hounds. The cows have to be penned, bulls separated and transferred to other pasture. That will take a full week.

Sitting in the truck looking out over the herd of mixed scrub cattle, Sam waits for the boys to show up so the penning can start. After sipping some coffee, Sam hears the sounds of trucks coming toward the pasture gate. The two men stepping out of their trucks ready for work seem excited and happy. Walking over to the horse trailer to get their mounts is a natural thing for Mike and Bryan. The only new thing is they have their own dogs. These are the sons of Sam coming to help with the cows. That is one big load of money off of the wallet, especially with the market prices down and feed mineral sorghum prices up. That was a good idea to plant feed grass in pastures just for hay.

Today the vet will come about 10 a.m. to test for pregnancy. Sam will hold back some calves and cull the older cows. The cows start moving toward the swamp, so Sam tells Mike to take Judy dog and his dog to stop'em. Then Bryan can come with the other dogs to bunch'em. They can ease them up to the penning gate lane and put'em in the big catch pen. Sam hollers to the boys, "You got your ropes?" Never can tell when you have to rope a stubborn heifer to keep her from going into the pond.

These bulls are big and tame. Sam can thank his dad for telling the tales back in Texas when he and his brother were drilling the first oil wells on King Ranch, one of the largest ranches in the world, Pop would tell of a herd of special breed of cattle that they were trying to develop, eventually becoming the Santa Gertrudis. Today they are the only North American registered cattle breed. Makes Sam feel like he was part of the same families living on the ranch, which is how he felt, although it was kind of silly. These registered bulls sure do work out well for Sam.

Bryan's horse is green and sort of skittish with bullwhips and lassos, so until he gets settled down, Sam would rather Mike took the point and he can just watch the back side for newborn calves. Mike began signaling to Bryan about one of the bulls. Seems like Ole 333 has some problem and Sam thinks that he's glad the doc will be here. Sam sure would hate to lose one of the original bulls. The last cow is in, so the boys swing the gate shut and climb up on the pen's side.

Mike says "What do you want to do first, Pop?"

"Let's separate the weanlings so they don't get trampled on and get hurt," Sam tells Mike.

Bryan jumps down and passes through cattle making his way to a side pen gate, after which he opens it slowly so everyone can move the little ones over and into the side pen safely. After that, Mike moves down the lane to check that all of the side pen doors are closed, after which he walks through the squeeze chute to check the big rear pen gate. Seeing everything closed, he returns and closes the chute gate then yells back that all is ready.

Only thing left to do is wait for the vet to come! Bryan and Mike take their ropes and start playing, trying to see who can heel a calf the most times. That competition was so intense no one noticed the vet arrive with his wife to assist him. As Joe climbed up beside Sam, he said laughingly, "Who's the winner?"

Bryan hollered back, "We don't keep score!"

Mike hollered, "Yeah, because he knows I'll win!"

Joe said that he would pull his truck outside of the pen close to the squeeze chute and they'll get to work. Jumping down, Joe yells to his wife Pam, "Bring the truck over here!"

After setting up and moving cattle down the lane to the squeeze chute, Sam worked the squeeze chute catch gate. The doc was testing Pam keeping records while Mike and Bryan did the herding, separating, spraying, and culling.

At dinner time, doc said that Pam had made sandwiches for everyone and brought some sweet tea. At the rear of the big pen, we all gathered to eat a sandwich and drink a plastic cup of tea while we talked about the market and prices. This is when vet doc Joe said that bull 333 would have to have surgery and that it shouldn't hurt his breeding. Sam thought he heard a big sigh of relief from the cows! Anyway, that's what it sounded like. Must have been the wind, though. Doc gets up and says, "Time to go back to work," as he opens the catch pen gate and returns to the front. Bird Woman carries the fern that she picked along with a spider lily that was growing in an old tree limb. Silently she moved down an old cow track through this cabbage hammock just below the ridge coming out off Boggy Bay. This is one place that a person can find peace while being in a natural state, along with all of the crawly creatures: snakes, gators, otters, lizards and such. All the while, Bird Woman enjoys nature's southern beauty. It's meaningless to a person who isn't born or raised in this environment. She loves wading through swamps looking for rare flowers to take back and establish in Spirit Woman's Garden in the yard. Life doesn't make everyone like or love the same things, except maybe a cold glass of water on a hot summer's afternoon.

When Bird Woman and Sam were fishing in the lake down by the swamp's edge, Sam had the pleasure to watch as Bird Woman, who caught a large mouth bass, taking it to shore to hang on a tree limb and then return to fishing. This is the same place that Sam catches eels and turtles which makes some pretty fine eating.

Home was located in a large oak hammock next to a small creek that wandered lazily into the Matanzas River. This hammock is where fruit and pecan trees grew along with berry bushes and in one corner was a flowing well. Just to the south a few miles stood Castillo de San Marcos and to the north stood Fort Mose for free slaves. Living in this area provided much in learning life's basics as well as protection.

Offering peace of mind to raise a family along with keeping to yourself, the Great Spirit gives gifts to certain people when they are born. To Bird Woman was given the gift of talking to birds and the birds would talk to her, thus her name. Together they could have made a spirited life. Sam Raven and Suz Bird Women, alike in most ways and enjoying most the same things.

Sam often used to dream in his younger years. Now the dreams are bad and cause his mind to flow through dangerous waters. Waters unmarked where no one has been before; knowing that he is the only one that travels there and only he can face the demons that try to kill him. These unseen private stealthy creatures living inside of his mind and body were put there in war and will only be released at death. At that time they will fly through space hurtle in the wind and romp with a breeze. Now only a woman can settle this plague to ease this strain of loneliness. Even though Sam tries, he just seems out of place without a good woman to help offset his feelings. Then his friend shall be nature and all of her loveliness.

Traveling through time is only to lean back, close your eyes, and journey on. Endless in time, place, things where everyone can reach perfection, do anything correctly without making a mistake and always win the race no matter the length or obstacles in the path. To have a goal seems a good start. Plotting the course to reach that goal creates dimensions beyond the realm at the time. Tacking to port or starboard may cause delay. Later it should prove the deciding factor in this journeyman's race for life's conquest for social goals, here in the world of mankind's wonders of today!

Thursday, Friday, Saturday, and Sunday will be Rodeo Week. Man, he can hardly wait! Mercy, he loves those quarter horses, the ones used for the cutting horse competition. Just watching the fluid motion and flow of the horse while it works brings grace and beauty alive in horse sense. This is a time for families to see old friends and enjoy the show. The parade will be downtown on Saturday afternoon and later that night, bull riding, bronc busting', calf roping, and barrel races can be entered for a cash money prize.

Copper, Sam's roping horse, came out of New Mexico, a glassy-eyed wiry palomino, which has more cow-sense than any ten cowboys that I know. Guess Sam and him will try for that money pool. Those ole boys are getting together back behind the cattle chutes.

Well, look over there! Seems like Suz and Nancy came dressed to dance! Wow! Sam thinks he's never seen anything more beautiful! He hopes they take some money home tonight. Those two girls really like to compete! Suz rides as if she's trying to catch the wind. Nancy rides as if she's chasin' the wind with only a second's difference in time.

Sam hears somebody call out his name. Turning around, he sees big Charlie riding over to say, "You're number three in first go 'round calf-roping, Sam!"

He just waves his hand, then turns to go back to the stock trailer to get his horse and ropes ready. Copper senses his time to shine like the sun's early morning rays which frolic and dance from leaves over a spring onto and across the tops of glassy waters in a mountain pool, disturbed only when a fish rises to take a nymph resting there leaving a cascade of never-ending circles only to fade away with time!

Breeze tells the tale of this Indian man called Blue Eyed Raven riding a blue-eyed horse roping a giant wind to save the tender birds and fowl of nature's home and not be killed for the evil one's pleasure, to remain for songs to sing for everyone to hear and to feel joy in their soul.

Thinking of being on time, Sam stepped aboard his horse to move into place for this event. First two cowboys were ready to go when Sam rode up. All of the others were just waiting their turn, so Sam puts a pig 'n string rope between his teeth, unrolls his lasso, and with tender ease, flips his arm twice to form a loop, sliding it under his arm to keep it from getting it turned. When it's in the air, it will settle over an object without knotting and coming out of shape.

The second cowboy comes out the arena gate, and with a smile, says, "Beat that time, Sam!"

As Sam gives a gentle nudge with his legs, Copper strides through the gate into the arena with a spirited nervous gate. As Sam backs him into the box, timing rope stretched across the front end, Sam looks ahead and nods for the calf to be released. His nose is the first thing Sam sees, when automatically he feels a lunge erupt from between his legs and Copper is halfway out of the box dead on catching that running calf. Sam with his arm lifting high as he flies past the chute gate, he swings one time and throws.

Before an instant, Copper is sliding to a stop, rope still in mid-air, and Sam half off the horse. Just then, the rope settles over the horns and flips the calf down. As the yearling calf is getting to its feet, Sam grabs it, lays it on its side, placing the pig 'n string over a front foot, pulling it tight with his right arm while gathering the back feet and pulling them forward, wrapping the three together with two hoops and a holler, hands in the air. Almost looked like somebody cutting a stick of cold butter with a hot knife.

Another horse and rider were next coming into the arena as Sam rode out. Sam said, "Go get 'em" as they passed. Later he would say "Way to go!" Sam didn't win, but he guessed second ain't bad. Sam thinks to himself that he'll mosey back to the stock trailer to get his horse brushed, put his blanket on, and give him some hay to munch. Then he'll try to find Bird Woman to see what she did; then maybe he'll get a hotdog with chili hot sauce and coffee. Then they can watch what the other guys are gonna do. He wants to watch the cuff 'n horse competition.

Last June when Sam was out west, he looked at a cuffin' horse that he thought about buying. He thought to himself, you know, money in the pocket spends real easy when ideas flood the brain, but after thinking about it, he figured now wasn't the time to invest in something that he could lose money on. Good thing. With economy down in the well right now, it looks like it might be the time to hold onto stock and not sell this year, he thought.

Pasture fed beef fatten just as well with good management for a year, then a few months' grain-fed before auction will bring top dollar. If he used part of the lower pasture to plant corn, buy a hammer mill, cut, grind, bag after harvest, he thought, well, just might make it! So much for dreaming here under the stars at a rodeo. They say cowboys dream crazy things!

A sweet voice says, "Slide over," as Suz easily slides in and sits down close to Sam holding a can of Diet Coke in one hand and a box of Cracker Jacks in the other. She said "Whatcha been doing?"

And Sam, who was short on words, said, "Oh, just working at the ranch. Been staying close to home lately. How about you?" Suz says, "Some friends came by and I have been trying to get the flower bed dug so I can plant some new flowers. Do you mind if I come out and get some tree orchids out of the swamp?"

"No," I replied, "There should be some in the bay behind the catch pen on Boggy Bay."

"What about along Hospital Creek close to your house?" Suz asked.

"No, I looked there already," Sam said.

"Too salty, I guess," replied Suz.

"It will be good to see you anyway. I have some new calves to show you and Ole Dusty needs to be ridden anyhow. Why don't you ask your sister if it would be okay if she took Charger back home and you came home with me? I could take you home tomorrow. Whatever you want to do," asked Sam, while he secretly wanted her to say yes.

Sliding out of bed the next morning, taking a shower, getting dressed, going into the kitchen to put on some coffee, Sam turned on the TV news to find the weather report. A person working with nature sure needs to have advanced warning concerning the weather.

Catching movement out of comer of his eye, Sam turns to see Suz coming through the kitchen door. "Coffee smells good," she says."

"Yeah. Ya wanna cup?" says Sam, while reaching into the cabinet where coffee mugs are kept. "Cream or sugar? I can't remember," he asks softly. Sure has been a lot of time since we were together," Sam added. "I guess life has its own plan for creatures two or four legged, and me and you," said Sam.

Suz looked at Sam and said, "I guess. Look at John Panther and Jewels Red Bird, how long before they got together and how much fun they have now!"

"I guess it's never too late," Sam said laughingly.

Suz says, "I need you to come help me redeem the floor in Spirit Woman's house. It is such a beautiful oak wood floor. I want to re-sand it ad re-stain it with a natural color. You might as well come over and help. Ya ain't got nothin' else to do," as she laughed that's what old Red Bird would say!

Back in the day, the first thing that would be done is to buy a case or two of beer and then everything would go fine. Maybe finish in a day or so! Never worry about tomorrow, just do what you can do today as long as the beer holds out!

Chapter 2

Back on the Black Bayou, where da crawfish and catfish are found, lives an old black man. They call Panther Jim. He's got yellow eyes and can see at night just like them big ole cats. A finer fellow can't be found around these parts and nary a town.

One time he saved some city folk from drownin' and soon to be gator bait when their fancy boat hit a snag and went down right there on Black Bayou! Panther Jim brought 'em to shore, give 'em a big feed, then took them to nearest outpost, and then disappeared back into thickness of Black Bayou. Story goes he's still there today!

This is the location where Bird Woman's sister lives and teaches little folk, those young 'uns born on a bayou near to the sea. Always looking to find a better way of life, lovin' to hunt or fish. Like they say "Don't let time pass you by. So let the good times roll."

High in the sky, soaring along nature's foremost spirit, flies in the form of a Black Raven, knowing all. Seeing the past as well as the future, this special one carries a sign of the sky marked in its eyes. Blue was the color of the earth when it was born, allowing creatures to see forever on a clear day; the mark in the sky to show a heaven far away. To reach it takes a lifetime journey of hard work to earn your way.

Sam knows these tales by heart, ones learned from elders around camp fires at night when the spirits would come in different forms. Sometimes it was an owl, others a bobcat or deer.

The Raven would sit on a gallberry bush to tell of things to come of light and dark to seek togetherness and not be turned aside; much like before sunrise or sunset there is a period of time known as the *Glow*, an in between time of togetherness before it is too dark to see, or in the morn when life is astir and newness is in the air. This blue-eyed sees afar future or past knowing that one day is but time past.

Tiana Butterfly talks with this raven of time past and things of the future testing to see how he came to know all of these things? Butterfly knows one day her turn will come to lead her flock in life's foray searching fields, meadows, hills and valleys of life to spread cheer, trying to feel this innermost compassion of togetherness described by many as an entwinement of souls bequeathed by living in the Garden of the Spring in a mountain stream creating a heavenly way for nature's keeper to take leisurely strolls across North America onward.

Early men created a barrier too high to cross traveled parallel to the coast into the country below, there to establish a dynasty to remain until men from across the sea came in search of treasure and gold where they pillaged and murdered all who to them did not respond quick enough, giving them the things they desired. Killing in the name of God to instill mercy and peace upon the heathen heads and wives! These invaders had cannons pulled by horses or mules. Men trained for fighting wore breastplates and helmets of steel and were riding horses, animals never seen here before, with swords and knives of steel wearing chainmail armor that arrows could not penetrate, with this train of horses and men taken by natives from camp to camp. They were greeted with favor, then left behind them fear, death, and pain.

A young native boy who lived in the village of Chieftainess Sonja Black Bear, close to the big muddy river that flowed to salt water, thought only how great it would make him be in the eyes of all the camp if he was to lead them on away from his home and children. When news came that these mighty white-eyed strangers from across the great sea were on their way, most of the food was hidden, because the runner said that they would take all, and he left to return home another way.

Traveling on through swamps and bog, this group of soldiers made better time after reaching higher ground. When they entered the camp of Sonja Black Bear, they were greeted as warriors from afar and given food and women. As the story was told, there was no gold or treasure held in the camp, for they were but farming people living on planted and harvested food, and hunting and fishing. They had young men that would guide them along their way. After days of eating all and collecting the remaining food stuff, these mercenary pilgrims enlisted to plunder and fight for riches and gold and returned home to be looked upon as conquering heroes, not the killers of a people with germ warfare through sex infected with syphilis, gonorrhea, and other such germs. These natives, not having an immune system strong enough to overcome such things would die when contracted from these men from across the ocean of blue. Catching a cold would kill a multitude.

Days of travel brought these foreign people deeper into the territory where native tribes lived. They never realized such individuals like these searched for a land they thought held the City of Gold, when they had reached far enough away from the camp of Sonja Black Bear. The young guide slipped away, traveling home yet another way so as not to encounter the men he had led away.

Seasons came and went before this train of warriors found their taste of gold. This went even farther into the caustic minds of gold. Lustful men creating a frenzy like no one wishes to have seen, much less be a part of, when mighty warrior men were killed. Beheaded bodies lay where they would fall, left to rot or be eaten by the dogs that these men brought with them as weapons of war. To behold such a sight brought fear to the hearts of many. To others it was a good day to die!

When the chief of the Nation was killed by these bloody men, the people retreated deeper into and higher into mountain homes secluded from many and closer to the heavenly. This is the place from which a beautiful maiden was taken to be a sacrifice to the spirit. Taken higher into the mountain peak by the holy men, fed a substance of berry juice to kill feeling in their body and were fed no food for days. They reached the top and she was made ready, then struck on the head with a killing blow wrapped tightly in sacred wrapping cloth, then buried in a sitting position to then become mummified by the cold, freezing ground. In this gesture to the gods, a good crop would be harvested and the people would survive another year.

These humans harvested a metal of gold, melted it, and made ornaments to portray and to adorn the chamber of priests or holy places of worship, plus were given as gifts to rulers of greatness as beheld by the people. For this reason, these foreigners have come. As these people captured or killed everyone who did not submit to their will, this Nation of People who built and ruled under leadership of a king were cast out and became wandering nomads settling in small bands under one chief of different nations such as Arapaho, Cheyenne, Sioux, Cherokee, Seminole, Crow, Apache, Delaware and many, many more thus this story begins.

Under one nation of Crow, the black bird people who lived to harvest grain for their crops with pumpkins and squash, with potatoes and corn, all to establish a mainstay for food in this new country from seeds brought with them on this journey of life; tomatoes and peppers were used in wickey-ups, tee-pees, Hogan's all! Shelters built or erected to use as home in the area where they chose to stay! Building, changing daily, following herds of the plentiful buffalo, plains natives used every part of the buffalo from intestines, internal organs, meat, bones, skin and fur. What they did not consume, they used for clothing or shelter.

This was a time that only they controlled between each other. Then came another influx of these hungry foreign men, this time bringing females with them so that they could stay. The ones that claimed to escape religious persecution floundered. Some were abandoned, while natives helped and taught others to survive by doing this much later, which caused their own demise by the same people they befriended and called brother.

Time passes, and with men unsatisfied with the things under their control, wanted more: To make their own laws to control their lives instead of paying homage to someone in control, paying taxes without representation was the cry heard around the world, and using the tactics learned from these natives, farmers took up their rifles and the fight was on.

After many battles and hardships galore, using tactics that were needed, the result was the defeat of the foe. Then was the time a new Nation was born.

Feeling big and brassy later in years, these men became profoundly irate when they could not own or settle on land that the Cherokee Nation owned. Again, war was waged on these Indians along with the Creek Nation. After years of fighting, some of both the Cherokee and Creek escaped into Florida and formed the Seminole Nation who never surrendered to anyone. While the Cherokee Nation was rounded up and forced to move into other lands, far off lands!

In protest, they chose to walk what is known as known as *The Trail of Tears*, to be settled on bare fields in this, the Indian lands of Oklahoma. To this day, some of the people not choosing to live like that broke away and lived where they may.

Ever present to all of this, the blue-eyed Raven sits taking stock in this day's process for this time and place. Leaving his perch atop an elegant cedar tree, the Raven takes wing, taking place to free slaves from indenture, to not work free or be someone's personal property that could be bought or sold, beaten, killed, or mistreated in any way.

This Civil War separated homes and families; a nation divided could not stand, as President Lincoln proclaimed. Thus, a time of very hard feelings raged on for many years with a very large count of maimed or dead men.

When a winner was decided, this Nation would then be brought together to become stronger than before.

The Raven's thought was interrupted during this ordeal, casting long dark shadows across many of the fields where brother against brother fought to the death! To rest for a while, the Raven flies across the wide blue Atlantic searching for peace and tranquility.

Decades pass and strength arose again. The world at war will interrupt human's life again with World War I, a war never to be fought again, in such places as Flanders Field was the war to end all wars.

Raven's path was interrupted once again, and this is with World War II. Taking note of this, Raven thought back through history how humans will gather to attack or maim others of the same kind. Why is the question instilled through grace and peace? To combat growth, I suppose. The answer will be just because of types of governing that doesn't allow certain kinds of freedom to be had. Alternating currents flow throughout mind matter in this sea of spirited humans, as frequency levels change due to the earth's atmosphere being bombarded with cosmic ions, neutrons, protons, and plasma, never regulated by nature; at certain intervals in history's timetable, to become a little erratic, causing the frequency waves to reach unattainable pitch, thus causing humans to go sort of "crazy" for a special reason that they think attainable at that point in time!

Revelations abound in thought and schemes causing humanity to purge itself periodically to remain on a steady path. Who knows, for humanity's sake, what lies ahead?

Ever so gently, the Raven drifts along throughout time and history to observe, to know, to keep in mind, then fly away and returning another day. Recalling faces of children in time, how they grew to achieve, what they have only because they were there in place for actions to implement for that reason at that time, never knowing what would take place on down the road of time!

Compare the past, by which I mean: How has humanity changed, other than having made things easier for accessibility in industry, life, and relaxation? It is no longer required to work from sunup to sunset in modern day countries, and because of this thought, it has turned to all countries being rated the same!

This is not the case for many people living under rule of a prominent head such as ruler, king, queen, chief, perhaps commissar or dictator? The rule of thumb has always been whoever is bigger and stronger shall lead and rule; to them are given the best of everything and they always had first choice in whatever prevailed, never taking the lesser or least, by demanding the most and best of everything.

Winds of trend sail closely to the ground creating difference to things when seen basically the same, only presented in a different way, creating an illusion to alter mood of mind.

Seasonal rains are starting to fall. This time of year is rather muggy and damp. With a full moon beckoning to lighten the way, time to take the hounds and catch wild hogs that are causing havoc outside their swamp domain.

Bryan, with a friend, gathered up the hounds, loaded them into the dog box in the rear of his truck and disappeared into the river swamp, catching wild animals at night with just his hands and a pocket knife. That takes knowledge, know how, and wit. Especially when this hog weighs about 200 to 300 pounds, has tusks that will cut you like a razor edge blade moving through warm butter, or will kill a dog without a sound after taking refuge in the middle of a large clump of saw palmetto. They can also tear through a man's skin leaving a bloody trail behind.

Traveling to the area where the hog sign was last seen, the dogs are released, running straight into the swamp following the scent trail that man cannot smell. Moving straight to the hog, a fight ensued where gnashing of teeth and popping of gums was heard coming from the hog. In an instant, this fight had begun between hounds and wild hog along this river bank called Matanzas, meaning "bloody slaughter" in Spanish, in the middle of a full moon night.

Quickly, Bryan runs into the thicket, knowing the danger of this wild hog cutting or killing his hound dogs. He's also aware of the danger to him if this hog knocks him down or cuts his legs. Not hearing the dogs, but hearing only squeals from the hog, Bryan realizes this hog is caught by the dogs. Moving cautiously and quickly towards the sound, he reaches through the palmetto leaves and wraps his hand around this big hog's tail, then giving a big heft, he lifts its hind feet off the ground, then hollers for his buddy to come quick to help him throw this big hog down!

With the weight of two healthy, strong men, this hog was finally flipped off his feet and lay on the ground with dogs still attached to its ears and with a white, bloody foam coming from his mouth.

Bryan tells his friend to kneel on the hog's neck so he won't be able to move his head while he ties its feet together so it can't get away. Then he tells his friend to stay with the hog and he will take the dogs back to the truck and get a stout hardwood pole to use so they can carry this hog back to a clearing, which is just a short distance away, where he can drive in the truck to save time.

After returning to the truck loading dogs, then driving into the swamp clearing, Bryan gets back to his friend as fast as possible. Together they carry the hog back to the truck.

This animal will be penned up for a few days for medication to be placed on the wounds so no infection will set in and then he will be ready for release back into another protected area far away from this place. Catching pigs and sows isn't that hard. But sometimes, on the other hand, a mother hog protecting her young can be a storm of destruction, especially if she is cornered and sees no way to escape.

Sam Raven travels side by side with spirits past, present, and future enlightening the paths crossed, broken or just not taken by humanity, so their way will be easier in the world beyond.

Chapter 3

Dancing happy 'fay do-do,' time to be relaxing to throw your cares away,
to another day or year when things will be mo' better then they is today.

People, friends, neighbors, and kin are brothers and sisters during
this time of feast. Nobody works on these days: just party, laugh and
have fun. The only thing required is to cast all of your blues away! Be
happy, revel, have fun, for such is custom down Louisiana way.

Louisiana, home to shrimpers, fishermen of all sorts and kinds
where the Cajun is country folk and the Creole is city folk and all other
are someplace in between!

Earlier, the Raven told of this magic place with black water sloughs,
black-haired, dark-eyed beautiful folks, happy children on the floor
playing with hound dog pups or baby raccoons, learning to fish before
they could walk, later to hunt, trap, live off of this land where nature
was hard at times but *Oh, so sweet!*

Late afternoon on Saturday, kinfolk would come around with a six-
pack of beer and a one-eyed dog; men folk would call the hounds and go
into the swamp looking to catch a 'possum or coon to fetch back home
and then cook it to eat. Mister crawfish was always around in creeks,
bayous, or flooded rice fields there to eat most of the time, along with
fish or gator tail. If a person went hungry, living there in the swamp, it
was from their own laziness, not from want.

Moon would get high-beaming through the live oak trees when the
men would come back singing a song, happy as you please. Then after
supper and everyone fed, they would turn on the radio, dance in the

kitchen until the morning sun shown from new dew-covered grass in front of the house, memories linger still with time at no end, and life's journey still a far piece to travel with no end in sight ... feelings without favor given to nature's own, spilling over in compassion, trust, and love.

In today's society whatever became of these? Petals of the rose flowers in spring and late summer, too! Over and over throughout eternity with planting of seed, a sprout will grow; from that shoot, a towering bush will grow. Then within that bush, different limbs will extend. From that, flowers will bud and then flower in beauty for all to behold. Life should take this lesson in stride, trying to emulate nature's own who give their all without asking to receive anything in return!

When left alone to survive, these plants live on for decades of time until an act of nature destroys what is there, and then with nature's help, rebuilds same again from roots that have taken a strong hold in the earth's soil.

Depending on a time given, aren't humans here on earth, supposed to be living life in beautiful gardens of celestial grace in peace with love? Riding out into the desert of life astride a strong beautiful horse with no name, this mighty steed can outrun torrential wind and rain. Hearts cascading from emotional waters running so deep, then bursts forth falling precariously onto rocky crags with boulders so eminent below them, settling ever so gently, softly, safely into the calm pool of heavenly grace. This is where you came into this world by being born.

Throughout many days of experiencing different things, to become aware of what and what not to do in life's length of days, to experience the touch of animals not like you, to feel the warm nuzzle of a newborn colt who is trying desperately to stand on its four wiggly legs, looking for something to eat from momma who is standing so near, looking at her newborn and knowing that someday he will be a champion to lead the way. Days pass as muscles of strength grow to carry it ahead of all the rest.

Higher up the slope of woods, a newborn litter of wolf pups were doing this same routine of learning and growing. By chance, two of these animals happen to meet without fear, which was learned from others. They smell each other and touch noses to say "Hello." Together they run and play until interrupted by an older animal of the same breed telling each to stay away, because they are not like you. So these two will part company, never knowing that someday they will see each other and meet again. As seasons change, wild animals flow to areas where nature provides food in abundance so that they may put on weight to make it through the winter's chilling winds and snow. During a bad winter blizzard is when enemies stay close together, giving each other space, and try to forage for enough food to stay alive. Higher elevation provides safety for big horn sheep and mountain goats looking down the valley provides a serene location for mule deer, antelope, elk with buffalo, too, all gathering for food during this winter's storm, as ravens sit among the tree limbs waiting for pine nuts to fall upon the ground, then with haste, they swoop below to eat this morsel that contains much protein. This will help sustain life through a hard winter's storm.

Flying on southeast, a life of a certain paint horse is changing from being stabled in a pasture, moving to a new home where it will be loved, cared for, and exercised each day.

As Bird Woman and her sister had a horse, so will this family, and the girls will ride, learn and accept responsibility for the care, feeding, and grooming. These things are part of growing up, making a person knowledgeable to nature's relationship with humans; how they work together to become strong, to fulfill a certain space reserved in your book of life especially for animals that you loved!

Calling energies that are reserved deep within a person's mind that relate to when you were a child seems somewhat more appropriate in raising children today, with time flying away trying, to teach the respect for life that you were unknowingly taught growing up with animals of all sorts. At the time, you just thought that it was all fun and play, riding your horse or petting your dog or cat. These animals always understood and loved you at all times, even when you mistreated them; like the time you tied a ribbon around the end of your dog's tail just to watch him run in circles as you laughed until he pulled it off; after which he would run over to you just to lick you on the face showing his love for you; and the times that you would dress your horse in all of his finery just to show it off in a parade or show in the same respect the care and time given to training for competitions so that you could be awarded trophies or ribbons showing that you were the best that day in that competition. Without a good animal under you, how would you win in that form of competition?

Raising animals as a child teaches understanding of these creatures and to love and respect their feelings, also their way of thinking, much like yours, but perhaps in a more defined way. Humanity is less defined in the respect of life, the more that you learn opens defined areas in life to access. Animals have the same access, but less interest in these things humanity depicts as worthy riches, and with this Holy Golden Metal, can rule the world! While creatures of nature feel the same way about living, only they are dependent on the natural growth in nature's earthly garden for length of days here on earth.

Humanity cares little for thought. They are born, live, and die, and what they do here during their stay means little to them or posterity, for in that length of days bequeathed to humanity, they wish to build giant structures to leave their mark after they have gone. This is believed to be as common today as in yesteryear. The fact is, have they really gone anyplace? Their Ideas are used over and over again in different centuries in different places with each new structure built; the basics are the same. Different material used is because of location and availability.

Chapter 4

Is humanity returning to the past simply because with the knowledge of today, the same building material is found to be the best, but with growth of population and misuse of nature's own, humans have tried to duplicate nature with synthetics, enzymes, polys and plastics?

Humans today built plastic trees, flowers, and shrubs to decorate places. Will the future provide a special plastic seed to be buried into the earth for growth of plastic trees? How about food? Will a body learn to survive eating things designed to save a body and not allowing enough natural protein to aid in physical growth, just mental growth? Thus the talking heads? More or less, the latter was used with tongue in cheek to show how today's follies will be used in the future, unless humanity becomes aware of things before they kill and eat their way out of a home here on this planet. Already they look for another planet to move to because of overcrowding with humans. Will this be a repeat of similar actions throughout history, only found today in a different century or different location? Or does history repeat itself still?

Maybe the original humans have not left, but only changed with time and place, learning survival past, present, future! Humans that have rejected advancement and still live by nature's means, as well as a little communication with modem man will be the ones that will start a new dynasty for humans after the *advanced* citizens leave to find a new home in outer space on a different planet far away!

As humans grow with age, so does their attitude towards life from rapid advancement, thinking time is money, to time devoted for relaxation so life's relevant beauty with animals, people, flowers, trees and things that you never really noticed on your way to the top in the world's daily routine.

Emancipation of your personal freedom to express personal thoughts *choose your life*! was foremost to many, never realizing just how fruitful life could be by just living one day at a time instead of hurrying, rushing, dashing to complete a deadline for goals set in your mind's eye, always aware that time could pass you by without so much as a hello or goodbye, just a being stalled in place here in earth's atmosphere, never knowing the full potential of your mind or body, just stalled on the railroad tracks in humanity's love to be run down, pummeled, crushed into bits and pieces, ground under foot without even crying out.

The past is brought forward in the mind, while the present is what you do today. The future is what can be seen in an unclouded mind brought about through knowledge, gathered in another time, space, and age. So you see, has humanity really left this earth or does time just repeat itself in another century and location?

The gift of giving was portrayed in forms not like the ever-growing religious realm today, one in which the act of giving is thought better than to receive, often delivered through interpretational plays read from documents or perhaps relayed in history, passed down from generation to generation.

The act of giving is really a commitment by another to say "Take this, a part of me, to show a commitment from me to thee."

Many times that commitment was broken by callous minds who only thought to enhance their position in the status portrayed in the world order of that day, whether it be in society or through financial gain, only to enhance their status symbol of that day, to have more than the other, often times speaks out in social verbiage saying, "I am somebody to be treated with utmost respect and a person in lesser status may not pass this way unless they acquire as much or more than me! Then I shall assume to be the same!" But in reality, they just feel jealousy of another having more!

The financial world is but temporary. So many people fighting to have all of the things that the one person holds doesn't give peace of mind, only loss of mortal soul found in humanity in all ways!

Taking stock of this situation, the Blue Eyed Raven flies on, knowing that someday it will see the same thing again in another place and time, only to witness unsuspecting humans trapped, mauled, and then devoured by the Big Fat Money Bear, who only lives for capital gain!

The love of two, a husband and wife, living a compatible life means more to the future than just playing the game of marriage, bringing children into this world that has nothing to offer but killing and greed, stopping actions of commitment totally one to the other for love, life, work, pleasure, heartache!

One caring for the other, then when a child is brought forward, to become one in raising and caring, for loving that child and so on, as the family enlarges; then when the first becomes aged and unable to help themselves, the order is reversed. The first shall then care for and love the older ones until they return to where they came. So go creatures of the wild. The rhythm is there, but only felt by certain individuals of the human race, the higher order in animals so they say.

Where will humanity be when this lack of knowledge proves the catalyst between eating or starving to death? When creatures during times like these have a way of sharing between different kinds of beast, knowing that is the only way all will survive, by working together in each one's own way to share the food so enough will be left for another day!

Nature's realm is never seen, only anticipated from the past; never knowing the future, only predicting what may take place; gathered from actions past and from the studies of scholar's past. No one knows the future!

So, fly on Black Raven, fly on! The song that he sings while wandering vacant salt marshes where at one time a vast array of creatures lived, today only outcropping limbs of myrtle bushes, with a series of giant cattails provide resting places for migrating fowl, soil poisoned from sewage, pesticides, petroleum coming from vessels using the waterway.

Beautiful animals and creatures of prey have long since left the area to live where there isn't so much careless waste and lives of nature's own are protected; not thought of as pests, something to drive away. As humans invade this home of nature, animals and birds today must move to live or be forever eradicated in the name of progress.

Sam sat hunched back against an old tree stump, just letting his mind wander through life's history maze, trying to imagine how many humans before him, walked across these same trails and let their mind track back thinking the same as he did; thinking not of things of that very day, but of things past and will they happen again someday, just maybe in a different way?

There are thousands of ways to make something die, some fast, some slow, but when you are dead, you are dead! Now comes the proposition of are you gone?

Death claims the body, but the soul is still in the air. You may have died and not left the area. Some think this is the same with animals as with humans. This is a dilemma that could be or maybe not, depends on the one that is contemplating this mystical tonnage of thought.

As a child, Sam Raven would spend hours of a day down by the water's edge fishing to catch food to eat, looking at nature and how it was being influenced by humans trying to contemplate the outcome.

Now after many moons, this story is again being told. The one of what was then shall once more take its original form back again in this world of nature, since humanity's effect is but temporary no matter the length of time! Grazing across this hidden pasture reserved for the portion in life that effects all from humans on down the chain of life to the most humbling cell is controlled by nature; humanity's field of dreams and what is common to you at the time. Stepping out of line when traveling a path in life's pasture causes turmoil, pain, and indifference, not to be confused with following a path to destruction!

When destiny beckons a young creature, it may be easily led astray to follow a hard, dusty, tiring road that leads to nowhere. But they can turn around at any time to return to the narrow trail that they were on originally, never losing anything but time.

Sam Raven knows that time is relevant, and whatever you are behind in today, tomorrow will prove generous, making all things equal. Traveling through underbrush, silently moving without delay, figure tall and slender, he talks with animals that he meets along the way. Whistling with birds, talking with skunks, raccoons, fox, cattle, and horses enlighten a path for this human along his journey down life's way! A hawk soars high above the treetops with a vision so strong that it may see the tiniest mouse under the grass below, then just as his journey finds an open space, Mr. Hawk swoops down to retrieve his meal.

Around a poultry yard, this hawk becomes the predator for humanity depending on these domesticated fowl for their source of food. Believing the weather to start turning bad, Raven searches for a hollow to rest his feathered frame to wait this storm out and let it pass, pausing no more than to replenish the dry river beds and natural cisterns for holding winter's melting snow or replenishing the ground water that has become low from use by humanity.

Sam watches intently, as deep in the tall grass that is tightly woven together forming a secret concealed cave, dwells a mother marsh rabbit that has just given birth to three tiny bunnies, their eyes are not yet open. They nurse from their mom and will stay totally dependent on her for the first few weeks of their life, after which they slowly start to determine their place in this wild rabbit family. Soon the does will grow large enough that they will pair off with another buck rabbit to form their own family a distance away. This is another natural part of natural animal's wheel of existence.

Then there are a few slight differences, such as the seahorse family; the difference here is that the male seahorse carries the fish eggs until maturity when they burst out of the pouch and seek refuge in grasses on sea beds.

Life beneath the waters of this planet are unknown to many. Life is encased in secrecy, only known by divers who venture into the vastness of inner space. Here the atmosphere is reversed from what is outside of the water field. For example, the weightlessness and the pressure of oxygen to breathe are but a few things humans or earthbound animals are not naturally made to live in.

Today in this century, given the right equipment, these things have been overcome to a certain degree allowing humans to operate and observe life that has never been seen before as it lives and functions daily. In doing this, humanity has lost a lot of fear of the unknown and the apprehensions of monsters from the deep told by various folk throughout time and embellished as ages past until they were believed to be true, which would frighten humans who would sail upon the sea, blaming shipwrecks on these evil tales of folklore, sea monsters, and demonic things. Or could it have been back in time when food was plenty here on earth and population was small.

At that time, vessels were smaller than these creatures of the deep. So, in reality, the stories told were true to a certain degree back then when things were built small to venture across waters deep, and blue creatures of the deep seldom seen were bigger in size than the vessels that humans traveled in, making way for rumors to flow, songs sung, stories told, all entertainment for humanity!

This is the revelation provided by looking deep into the Raven's eye, holding and seeing all. Fear unseen, mirror of thought, only to be made relevant in action! Finding that your fears were not really anything to be afraid of at all, only in your mind, where these things are made so terrible.

Facing the truth is made harder through a human's ability to know right from wrong. Humanity's action towards righting a wrong is called justice, which is swift and deadly, measured in degrees of culpability weighed on the scale of justice that rests in courts of man. In each court, there are different degrees of liability of wrongness that must be proven beyond a shadow of doubt before that human may be sentenced on the scales of justice! Throughout history, these same scales have been used over and over so many times that, in society, some judges or others in the measuring room have found a way to place their finger on the scale, when weighing, to allow it to tip in the direction they want it to go therefore allowing innocent humans to be prosecuted, serving time behind prison bars, or be executed.

The Raven sees these people and, in observing all, does not comment. He just files away, this action to be reviewed another day when those wronged shall seek their revenge administered in self-judgment and death through that person's own hands, for it is said, *in sin the results are death*!

Through the ages of humanity, these same humans in different centuries study history, and in doing so, repeat the same exact type of crime only in a different way. Is it seen to be different, because a different method was used in a different time. The results are the same, even if they are hundreds or thousands of years apart.

So, again this Raven puts forward the question: Has this person's body died, but their soul is still in the area and journeying worldwide doing the same thing wherever it goes?

Crime is crime in this world of civilized humans, today just as it was in history past, with the only thing changed are the ways of carrying out punishment, in some nations harder and some nations less. The difference in location and advancement are the factors given in weighing of the scale of justice. The crime committed is the same justice rendered not!

How does this affect the *moral majority* worldwide and why? Is it because a country that distributes less punishment for crimes committed is more attractive to the ones that make their living preying on honest humans without the chance of being caught and punished as severely as they would in their homeland?

Chapter 5

This is but one of the forms that fear may take inside of a human mind in which it attacks and takes control of trying to lead in a direction down a path that leads into foggy desolation where there is no end and only pain given in reward. When a human enters on this path, a helper is given to either turn that soul around and return back to the right track or join that soul on their destiny down that endless road of guilt and shame.

Records have been kept for a reason. Is it to show direction to others of things *not to do* or is it to be used as a reference book to expand upon, to refine, to experiment with alternative ways in committing the same actions or crimes?

Always knowing what the results will be before the act is committed, why does the mind of this human try to carry out this action? Then after receiving the prescribed results, say, "I don't know why I did it," or passing the blame to the unseen medium known as the Devil, lord of all unrighteousness prescribed on humanity.

Why don't these self-proclaimed intelligent beings find heaven or hell and devil to be in same body of the person that is committing the action at that given time? In one being, like Jesus said that he was: the Father, the Son, the Holy Spirit!

As humans say, "One night a devil, next day a saint." Or "The devil made me do it!"

For humanity, they need look inside their own minds and set the course of their daily actions that will either give longer days here on earth or cast them into a recycling bin to be issued later. Without reproduction today, that model may be replaced and no longer issued in that form or likeness!

Human animals are fun to observe, never knowing what to expect. Or an action taken at a given time shows the amount learned before! As two infants together, when one does something to the other, what action will the other take, *if any*, toward the offender. Actions are learned, not inherited through birth. Only genes that give way to learning, as well as intelligence, are inherited from childhood to present. Actions are taught, learned, either good or bad. Whatever that human species does throughout its existence is derived from observing and daily practice.

With a frigid gust of air blowing into its face, the Raven lifts its wings, taking flight once again, gliding through currents of air coming from the north wind, blowing across frozen ice atop of the earth's northern-most magnetic pole. this signals most fowl to fly south where it is warm, then return after the cold has returned home once again back to the North Pole.

James Jumping Frog, brother to Cecil Running Horse, has just returned back from a fishing trip where he would catch enough fish to eat and some to dry for use later.

Take the Nations ... in higher country close to the blue ocean, every year a certain kind of fish will come back to the stream where it was born. This is the time to catch enough for the winter days of cold when the rivers and streams are frozen over and the snow is high, making living a hardship at that time.

Raven sees how man mimics the ways of animals and how they survive. Time is what controls actions in nature in places where humanity has not tried to control the environment and structure places where man is, but is a part of someplace that he has not made.

Nature is where humans are allowed to live if they can abide by the rules of nature, not rules of man, where oftentimes bigger is better and strength determines power to kill or be killed is rule of the day. Often, it is found that in running away, you live yet another day. When leaving home, a young male must find a home and area of his own. This takes strength and cunning, combined with agility and skill.

What about the ones who don't measure up to these necessary things? They tend to remain in a bachelor group or become loners, not being allowed to reproduce so that the strongest, the best shall procreate and ensure the bloodline to survive.

Thinking that if the world started with only two of each species, how do you think that all of the different subspecies were formed? Take bears, for instance. If there were two bears, a black one and a white one, they copulate, and then a brown bear was born, and so on and so on, just as humans! Did the world start with two white bear and two black bear, male and female, or just two bears? Perhaps back then everything was neutral or the same color, and throughout time have been changed, their choice of locations and environment being the deciding factors in body color and tone. This is a dilemma to most educated humans, because without being there, who can tell with absolute accuracy?

It was once said that a person who knows everything doesn't know anything! Again, this is taken from humanity who claims to have intelligent people in the world of nature. These creatures that are alive today were here first. Or was everything created spontaneously as in POOF, new world is formed, and this is what shall live here.

In doing so, what has the power back then as in today, for the Raven is aware that something must control the future of and destiny of humanity! The Raven can only observe and retain thought past, present, and future never uttering comments, just flying on.

Dreams of today are but that! Dreams of the past today become a reality in many ways. Others are still trying to be perfected, for the growth of humanity here on this earth has expanded greatly and is about to overrun this confined living space in which humanity resides; therefore, searches have been cast into space, looking for a planet that will support life such as we have here. Then humanity may start all over again in another time and place in this outer space? Different humans in different periods of time studied the heavenly galaxies, all having different reasons, or is it because the rotation of the earth within this galaxy creates different basic things, such as seasons, the rise and fall of the tides, night and day, and gravity.

In the simple thoughts of animals, are these things ever contemplated or is life just too busy for them trying to live, eat, raise a family or care for their young while humanity is running wild?

Late evening shadows descend causing closed minds to open, emitting pure thought, not being led or influenced by anything or anyone! Just trying desperately to put personal thoughts into the memory banks of beings, alike in mental capacity, different in action or species. The area of location does not defer like thought as "I think." In one part of this world, so, too, may others be thinking the same as, but in different civilization lifestyles and location?

Wavelengths in thought, Raven believes, travel through space much the same as radio or sound waves. Humanity has harnessed these, but is baffled by mental telepathy because of charlatan carnival hucksters, wizards of magic, et cetera.

When two people of the opposite sex become one, each starts to think like the other in length of days, together, but separated by distance. How do they know through feelings that something happens to someone or thing over a distance which is immeasurable or endless? Humanity passes this off as being in love.

The Raven knows the answer, but cannot utter. Why? The Raven is only to observe, then fly away into the blue sky, lining its way into another classic problem found worldwide and locally, always the same, only in different locations, different civilizations, but basically the same! Humans are a breed that acts differently in separate locations with different actions, but the same results.

Back to the mental thoughts of mind and their projection, through these tracts of thought, humanity has tried to study and act upon, duplicate without being able to control, mind over matter or mind projection as studied worldwide in many different civilizations throughout noted history. Was this mind control used in any period of time before humanity's current civilization?

Hypnosis is used today. Was this used to control or overthrow multitudes through religious beliefs, actions, or rumors; with advancements in technology, today the same type of unholy individuals using tricks to entrap humans through tales, rumor traps using mind control through hypnotic constant pleading, preaching in constant droning sounds accompanied by sharp hypnotic sounds from musical instruments?

At the same time, keeping individuals confined in a stationary area for long periods of time, creating minds to be influenced with hypnotic mind control ... is this healing or hurting humans?

Humans can act on their own! As Jesus said, "Physician, heal thyself!"

As I interpret this action, the Raven sees when this philosopher/prophet/holy man Jesus traveled and taught man was made in the image of, therefore with the power of thought given to each mind, they have the power to move mountains through thought in personal ability. It's like saying if you think you can do something, you can!

The Raven uses different humans throughout time to represent actions in thought and actions at that particular period in time. Like the noted human of oriental precedence at a given time was Confucius, scholar of thought. Did these noted humans of time repeat tales of history handed down? Tales who were expanded upon, given personal claims, projected forward for that time period, and do those same words mean today as they did in the past? Has the basis of life really changed that much; to apply these same actions given ages earlier to be projected the same today?

Each generation says surely the end is at hand, glory of will come through rapture, and all believers shall rise together into heaven to live forever in the sky!

Did anyone ever think that the point given is to believe! To believe in yourself, to believe in your actions, and to believe that you can do whatever you think you can creates peace of mind to many individuals and this peace of mind is considered heaven!

In achieving this train of thought, wouldn't a person be living in the proverbial heaven here on earth? Again, speaking of the rapture taking place on earth, could that be interpreted as rapture of the mind when people start thinking in the same direction and their lives will be given an easy path to follow, one that exudes happiness, togetherness, and love, rising up in rapture?

It could mean that feelings of your status or station in life would be far greater than you perceive it to be at present. Not placing individuals into categories because of race, creed, color, or thought. Seeing individuals as just that. An individual ability to perceive is not allocated to certain humans with certain skills.

Perceiving is sowed through the seeds of humanity like wheat is sown with the wind that everyone shall receive as much as the adjoining person. The only thing different is how each shall use that given trait in life's journey down the path chosen.

Ability is another trait endowed to all. How each individual uses their given trait can be more or less in any form. Ability is a natural trait, and perfection is gained through training or repetition. The better you are at something is perceived to be acquired through doing the same act over and over again to gain perfection!

Although the society of humans rises up the act of perfection due to long-given periods of time in training designed for that one goal, to be the best at a given time, knowing there will eventually be another; for time does not stand still. Your body grows older constantly when awake or asleep, and even after death, portions of the human body still grow. From the time of conception until a memory, you are alive or dead. Before time when you were but a gleam in your parents' eyes, or a thought in your mother's mind, you were growing. After death, when just a memory? You are growing still as folk tales will tell. Growing still larger after death than before!

Still the Raven knows truth behind all tales told by fantastic storytellers around campfires or before a warm fireplace hearth when keen ears are tuned, listening with undivided attention given to aunt, uncle, mom, dad, or cousin Tom telling another fabulous story that you know is exactly true, for if it wasn't, they wouldn't have told you! Later in length of days and moons, speculation is raised *back to those days*, rendering thought of truth given to those words of wisdom given so many years before.

When, as a child in solitude, nothing around for entertainment, tall tales were told for pleasure and excitement for young folks at hand, the truth stretched a wee bit, making a true story so much more interesting for youngsters at hand, knowing that a big blue ox surely did pull a giant plow from the Great Lakes to the Gulf of Mexico for Paul Bunion to make the Mississippi River of today!

Days of childhood are filled with adventure, whimsical fun, and laughter with play. Isn't it an awful feeling to one day awaken to find that your body has grown too large to again venture into those tight places so convenient for tiny mites to explore or to hide in boxes and barrel empty of their contents that made the most perfect place to stand off the horde of wild savages that attacked your fort. Your fort as you defended it so gallantly and became hero, of course, for saving the town.

Humans are generally a great bunch to observe as they take charge of their lives and set sail on their own, then raise a family so that their linage will not be lost or perhaps compromised in other's thoughts, but not forgotten throughout time and history when humanity can trace their family history to find their roots in a way to give meaning and understanding to their life today.

Leaning on or riding on the coat-tails of others, whether past or present, doesn't say much about the person or persons riding, sliding, hanging on this slippery slope of hazardous times, trying to use the *courts of justice* today for actions taken in the past when they were not illegal. Is legal falderal given precedence today because of nothing more trying than past actions? If so, then what about descendants of the multitudes taken captive and made slaves during ancient days or periods in time of war?

Could this be a tactic used towards using mind-control starting to change the way humanity retains their desired way of governing a nation? Raven observes, knowing full well, that only humanity can and will control humanity no matter how much it hurts the things given to keep this planet alive. Humanity cannot outsmart Mother Nature, knowing she will prevail in the end!

Chapter 6

Without dread of deed, hunting the wild boar is in mind this day with hounds afoot and you by their side looking to capture this beast of prey; sport is found in man against beast, armed with nothing more than a stick and use of his mind in thinking how and when to act in close quarters in this fight, preferring not to get injured or causing damage to the beast. All of this done for relocation, doctoring, and release of said beast to once again find rule, its domain, living life to the fullest for that particular wild boar beast!

Returning to the old outpost, his home, the man retires into his favorite place of contemplation and relaxation, the bathroom or water closet, while taking a shower, washing away all memories of this day of trifling times, escaping into the smooth feeling as warm water cascades over and down his body, giving newness to life's mood, a mood as though entering a new, clean room after a tiring physical dirty area was left behind, altering and believing righteousness to be at hand. Every moment delivers suspense and excitement with various flickering thoughts of what could have been.

Now starting life anew, what will it be; as this trail has not been traveled many times before, so maybe those wavelengths between me and thee are working still.

Although they are only used in times of necessity, as certainty provides during times of need or stress when a close friend or companion is needed to talk to, maybe to confide in concerning something of a personal nature that you feel you can only be understood by the one who knows you as well as you know them, such as sharing mutual feelings and thoughts, having feelings the same as ones with like genes, reacting to likeable actions, smells, humor, music, alike but different; same as in thought, unalike in looks, stature, and movement.

Times when crying out "Lord help me" flies through your mind as scenes of past happenings flash into view, realizing that you're alive to try again causes instant repression, as quietly you return to life trying *not* to remember. Sliding memories back into the box in back of your mind and closing the lid, never knowing when they shall appear again or at what place or time, so you just try to stay away from humans. Just live with nature's throng of creatures, never accusing, trying to survive in life's turmoil of have and have not; have not portion is being delegated to the wildlife of nature by taking their food and homes, converting them into fields of recreation and homes to house humanity. Thinking that they will survive how? Humans use and overuse until everything is depleted, then move away, leaving behind all used structures and residue, never considering the animals that once lived and flourished in that same place before they came.

Listening to a local orator of the Baptist faith, a preacher is what he was called, teaching from a text taken from a book concerning a man executed, buried, then rose again after three days, taking life so that he may come back another day. But if he did not leave, only in thoughts of mind, then he is still here today!

To return at any given time that a mortal chooses to call upon his name, although he may appear in various forms such as your close friend, a person that you have only met a short time ago, or someone that just happens to be there at that time and extends a helping hand, never knowing why or expecting anything in return, for surely such is the Kingdom of Heaven here on earth?

The other important structure that makes things happen are made through the diligent actions of the woman always there to help a man, bearing children, and working tirelessly, strength untold, only for the love given in return, trying in all ways to please the man and keep him satisfied. She would gladly forfeit her life for the life of her offspring.

It's taken from the Bible passage "As the father has loved me, so I have loved you. Live on in my love!"

Surely innermost thoughts direct actions taken by humans in taking the role of a priest or leader of certain religious orders, expressing their belief, and practicing in their own personal way, and not controlled by politics either local, national, or worldwide.

There surely is but one Supreme Being, only worshipped in different ways by humanities various social orders and cultures. The human beast has always known the answer!

With natural actions, the Raven moves off in flight observing all in day or night. Believing the fact of life to be most relevant in society today as it was in times of past, so, too, will these things thought this day come to pass in future days in slightly different ways? From stockpiles of history stories being kept for study to learn and expand upon to find another new home far, far away.

Starting life again from basic life through eons to present, you might say doing it all over again, repeating learned actions again in a different time, date, and place! Life, you do it over and over again until you get it right!

Being cleansed from sin is through immersion in water, washing away all sin held within, making a newly reborn human to come forward, changing former habits to ones of a newfound friend's actions, raising you from the depths in this pit of shame to elevations wished for in life; today, to being respected by your fellow man, to have a tongue of righteousness, not one of defeat, to love your neighbor, thinking not of greed, a constant helping hand to those in need, telling others that you see traveling that path to nowhere and destruction how to return to the trail that leads to a path that is right ... even a better life.

Isn't that what all humans seek? To find their place in life here on earth so after they die and their spirit has flown away, to find peace and tranquility in heaven far away?

Another thought is working towards the peaceful tranquility found here on earth today, in the heaven built into each and every mortal's brain, overshadowed by teaching violence that doesn't come naturally; for in as much as what humanity has, and progression is inevitable, it seems doing so naturally will let humanity survive longer, while preserving the creatures in this garden of life! Let the natural order of things progress without humanity's interference in controlling, copying, or duplicating nature's own creations.

Human was formed in the image of and with the same powers, but how those powers are used will determine his length of days here on this planet. Nations of early humans have not changed or disappeared, just evolved and are constantly doing what was done at the beginning of time, only more things have been developed, making life less hard for some. The fact is that really nothing has changed. Babies are still being born, food is still required, water is needed to drink, death happens. Two of these, food and water, are becoming less and less each day. Is this just the natural action to reduce humanity to a number that can survive?

When and if things again revert back to start, will all things be as history tells it, when life started here on earth, when creatures were large, humans small, and food plentiful? Something major came to pass causing havoc to the largest of all animals. Was it lack of food? The environment? Air? Or a combination of all? Are these animals still among us today, just merely evolved through time and, due to shortage of food, have become smaller in size, like those omnivorous animals called T-Rex in dinosaur terms.

Today herbivore and carnivore exist in peace, each remaining in their designated place within the garden of earth. As saintly wings silently within normal currents of humanity, space, and heredity, the waves pound constantly upon the shores in the bay of genes causing a fluctuation, slight as it may be, to interrupt the journey of thoughts in a person's daily life! This slight movement causes a perfectly constructed mortal to be out of sync with reality for given periods of time. Lack of needed herbal substance causes a malfunction in humans, where riding on rails while traveling down the way of life with proper food as the guide, operating a perfect machine during its period of operation here on earth.

The journey of the Raven has given pause to see beauty given as well as other things. Topmost are feelings ... those things that are controlling actions as well as thoughts inside a frame, as on the outer structure of a mortal's covering. Feelings are emitted, carried distances through the unlimited void of space. Unknown are actions ... do feelings have to be expressed before meeting or do feelings travel without knowledge, just a realization that something or someone someplace is trying to tell you something?

Oh, the realm of life's cluster is constantly changing, causing this thing called life to be ever-active, never-resting, a constant, constantly moving from start to finish; then do it all over again, changing this and that, but a tad or perhaps a skosh, making it a little easier this time.

Has humanity been doing the same things since the beginning of time? Has a mortal ever thought that far back? Does anyone care to return to times of hardship, as they were back then? Maybe times were only hard for the humans that didn't take time or didn't care! Raven says, *Let these through, to travel on to their destiny, for after the die is cast, first shall be last, last shall be first in this thing called life, and who really knows, maybe these mortals are on a wide easy path to nowhere!*

Flapping its wings to land softly upon this ground, Raven begins to take in some fine morsels it has found lying among drying husk residue left after the harvesting of this field so green, of which is offered to animals of all kinds. After filling its empty stomach, Raven again seeks a place to rest, relax, and ponder traveling further on.

Meanwhile, back in the grasp of nature's large hand, portions of the earth are being blessed. Yet still other parts of the earth are being tried with sickness, the lack of food, water, death, the recycling of mortal frames simply for principles of feelings or actions. Ones that have the most shall receive more; the ones with the least shall have theirs taken away and given to the one with the most.

In the world of nature, the same principle is used, perhaps with more understanding. The lion, the king of beasts, makes a kill to ease its hunger pangs, and in doing so, all in the food chain of creatures are rewarded from the top down to the lowliest of organisms. Even birds of prey, cousins to the Raven, eat at this meal on nature's table, found here, in this earthly garden of life. Reverence is given to planetary solstice, solitude for beginnings of new life held in worship by early humans, knowing, but choosing to celebrate life in a different way.

Beginning the same, ending the same; what is in between creates tales to tell, another day by newly born humans in the same place, a different time, same lives evolved in time, same as animals here on earth. Humanity with the mind to see what will become of those that search for eternal life.

When they realize that it is constant from first to now, all are the same, just different attitudes throughout their period here on earth, when they die, their spirit is transformed into a new child born in that family. All men can trace their start back to the first, same is for women, here on earth.

Mind travels are such that a sense of forever is but a flash of the mind, a thin curtain between now and then. Behaving in time with rhythm, played with golden harps in nature's orchestra, found secluded within garden's gate deep into prime forest of celestial dreams with lovely flowers growing wild, emitting their special bouquet, captivating celestial moments in the mind's green meadows, enjoyed in the company of your chosen one, your companion, sharing moments in despair or joy, combining two into one for the livelihood and regeneration of life as humanity knows it today.

After which the time has passed for woman to regenerate life, then is the period of companionship dearest, just having a friend to share in life and life's daily happenings, to be shown love that remains unchanged, knowing that the chosen one seeks not the companionship of a younger breed for self-satisfaction or child-rearing; again, knowing that the best is the first and no one shall be beyond only doing the same thing in their own personal way. Life is again repeated, but still the same.

Plotting your course on the map of life requires moving right and up within a designated area at that time. With a mathematical protractor, you then cross and intersect lines from given degrees of longitude and latitude to give the position that you are in at that time in your life; then with a simple calculation of measurement from your given position to the goal you are trying to reach with length of time and distance, all of which is dependent on plus or minus life's rewards or hazards thrown in, good or bad breaks. You will have a very good idea of your life at any given time within this maze of humanity here on earth. Or reaching your goal before you die, then is the time to ask yourself if it is really worth it?

Simple though it may seem, dealing with humans is not all that keen. There are those that think they own everything. Then there are the ones who just wish to get by, while still yet some want to be left alone.

Humans are fun to watch in this earthly confined bowel of creatures, everyone pulling in different directions. It may seem, then again, what may happen if all were moving in the same direction after the same thing; the ones in the back trying to get ahead, while the ones in the middle are being trampled, and as the leaders tire, they are sucked into the masses and relegated to be in the rear, or perhaps try to regain a time to lead once again?

Looking into the eyes of humanity leads directly to their soul that tells who or what mystery unfolds in every aspect that follows shapes of features, types of skin, and color of same, changing with season, height, width, weight, age, and knowledge contained inside their mind held in a given frame.

Searching souls is another medium available to the solitary creature of humanity. In other words, only you can see inside of your personal soul when alive! After death, all is the same. On earth, mortals ask if animals have souls. Why not? They have the same as humans, only located differently and with their own forms of communication, having two eyes, nose, ears, reproduction organs, mammary glands, and brain ability! Babies are the same, with habits of survival being different!

Moving clouds around to arrange them in patterns of your choosing with mind control is but a thought. Do creatures have this type of power if full use of their mind was used? So many questions, answers are few at this time. What the future holds for the destiny of humans here in this garden of life located here on Mother Earth, of which the first natives thanked through worship, practiced in festivals and feast dances, thanking the *Great Spirit* for another good year of crops, meat fish, and fowl given them to survive.

Seeing these actions in the start of winter, the Raven is to observe worldwide celebration of the new year as humans celebrate the passing of the last moon and rededicate their efforts toward having a year of prosperity in their daily lives.

In earlier years, citizens of the village or town would celebrate having a good season for crops to grow and flourish. Alas, the humans would live through the winter looking to the next year for the sun to smile down upon their lives, allowing life to remain in that place, growing and expanding to what it is at this point in time.

Chapter 7

Humans, like animals, follow the chain of food. When one area has been cleared of substance to maintain life, they move to a place that has plenty of nourishment growing wild and free without control! After man moves in and settles down, more of the same arrive carrying a dream. After a while, from camp to cabins to town, state and federal controls are instilled to monitor the use of what is considered nature's provisions, there for creatures not alike to eat and survive!

The Raven sees that the controlling factor in humans today is a thing called "money," exchanged in paper derived from trees to represent gold yellow metal, for which humans kill to possess. The one with the most controls nations, people, and food. This worldwide area has different types of governing, almost like from beginning of time when someone would be chosen to be the overseer of the camp, village, or town.

It's the same today, only different in some ways that allow citizens a voice in the way they may live and how much they may ask for in payment when selling their possessions, either handmade or grown. Early natives used wampum in trading. Earlier civilizations had their own ways to exchange goods for goods in order to live.

Through the eyes of a deer moose, horse, or cow that graze the grasslands, what they see is food to eat, not whether it is owned by humans by placing posted signs on fence posts of private property farms or ranches. These animals living on nature's fare feed when and where they desire. One day they graze their way into an old territory, but find obstacles placed in their way. They either graze around that object or jump over it to feed on the other side.

Humans who plant to harvest that ground, kill to survive when they depend only on money they receive to pay another human to live on Mother Earth! Animals fight to break into this world and take their first breath on their own. From that point on, they fight to stay alive, depending on their needs. Through education, these needs are made easier to have. Humans are totally dependent on nature's actions providing life, giving rain, air to breath, food to eat. Living naturally is an everyday occurrence here on this earth at this time, date, and place situated in this point in known space.

Humans then act in various ways to proceed to enhance their actions in survival, attacking others that have in order to relish in spoils of war, to establish their longevity here on earth, and to maintain their dominant role in that place of time. These various forms of creatures depend on each other unknowingly, at the same time, trying to live and maintain their personal lifestyles in this ever-changing environment.

The Raven flies among the world being not of the world, while being in the world: observing, cataloging, filing, leaving signs of actions taken and actions to come!

A butterfly emerges from the transformation process it has undergone from worm to nature's delicate winged creature of flight, resting lightly on different flower buds, while taking nectar for nourishment and then flying away in search of more nourishment. Tasting of many creates nature's fertilization towards creation by pollinating buds. Thus, the knowledge held by the butterfly contains unlimited information of this Garden of Eden brought forward to give life a way to sustain life for another season of the moon.

Chapter 8

Tiana Butterfly soars in my mind as something so special words cannot explain; coming in times most needed, speaking truth through spirit and days happening. Together in service while walking through the clouds, talking with spirits in the winds to guide the way as we traveled this devil's road, knowing that death and destruction could meet us at the end!

To be prepared to live or die gives power to the brain, a sense of a job to be a job well done. No more, no less, only to do this thing that you do best at this place, at this time, then like a ghost to fly away! These *special forces* people are never seen unless they want to be. Much like the *Skin Walkers* of the *Nation's Medicine Men*. Some special ones possess power to transform into an animal or a bird, taking shape of whatever is around; "*Shape Shifters*" is what they are called by some, while others just hide their eyes in fear.

In ease of mind and soul, a story is told of a warrior who journeyed to the ends of this earth to face an unseen evil spirit causing pain and fear of death within Nations here on earth. As he traveled along the way, he found a great bald eagle with an injured wing. The warrior said to the eagle, "I tarry here to fix your wing so you may glide high in the sky."

After fashioning a splint from a nearby tree and strapping it on the eagle's wing, the eagle thanked the man, and began to fly away. Then with abounding joy, this eagle suddenly flipped around to alight softly on the ground. Speaking clearly to the Warrior, the eagle said, "Climb onto my back and I will carry you to wherever you must go." And in so doing, they flew off into the night.

This story goes on in adventure, days telling of faith so true, of going towards a goal with problems that you will be able to overcome! Mountains will step aside when you know the way! By helping a creature survive when nature's own family shouts loudly that a person's size is measured by their smallest deed to a creature in need, whether fish, fowl, or beast. Love shown to the least of these gathers love from the greatest of same to offer its help to you in times of need!

As I gather myself back into the space of reality, memories flood vast oceans of kinetic energy held in my mind. Times when Butterfly flew close to Raven's side, supporting air below its wings, assuring that no hostile force would come to either of them. Now, today, in this hectic world's pace, two have made a bond few understand. Raven promised to watch over and warn Butterfly from its place in the sky and Butterfly is to remain close to the earth, where safety is found.

After returning home from across the sea out of the desert, Storm Butterfly was hurt one foggy morning on a mountain road that caused her to journey in a different way. She was asleep for many days, yet taxed not beyond her will. Butterfly is rebuilding anew, living from day to day with three felines she adopted when they were in need of a loving home. From a time of despair to having a goal leads different people and things in different ways. While on the same path from death and despair to life or from life to death and despair.

Help comes for those in Sam's tale from the power above; the Blue Eyed Raven knows all and is able to see into the future as well as the past, casting grace where it may help creatures in need of special things, in times of need or deed that prolongs, enhances, or sustains a life.

After four years apart, Sam locates Tiana living in Ft. Collins, Colorado. Apart in stature, alive in spirit, connected in mind with fate, register a day and time when happenstance besets journey of these two. Fate brought one to the other, so they will pass surely on the everlasting highway through a mirrored valley of shame. One certain action that only you know of and everyone will face on this road they pass through in some portion of life, showing clearly to you through remembering of discretion that only you know and have never revealed to another soul. Privately placed in a safe area way *in the back of your mind.*

Surely as winter shall bring snow, here in the Rockies, times of happy bliss with you and all that you represent presents itself, happy with a certain glow around your form, a glow that is an aura given to you in nature's book, good simple truths found by a few, only those with a heart warmed by a hearth built within, a nether home that fears do not enter, nor mortal pain. Power controlled by you ...

One summer's day was a grand setting for Butterfly to take a mate. The one she chose to share her life was strong and intelligent, like stories of old. They met while doing their prescribed work, engaged for the certain time for love to aspire, then were married in Loveland, Colorado in the Rocky Mountains, high in the sky where the air is clean, life is fresh, and each day is anew with the spirit inside of your soul causing happiness unexplained.

Best of all that Raven has the pleasure to know is that it only takes a few seconds to open profound wounds in those you love and it can take many years to heal them. Eagles soar above the mountain stream where the wolf dog likes to run and play in the winter's new fallen snow, so soul white and pure to the touch. Reaching down, you gather a handful of nature's frozen heavenly moisture. This gift from earth's father helps replenish the creek water to quench thirst of desert lands on which creatures live and survive. Spires of a Giant Saguaro cactus bears a beautiful yellow flower that offers sweat nectar for hummingbirds and butterflies.

Raven sits atop resting from their day's journey. Here in this mountain meadow, where grasses grow high beside a wandering stream home to animals, creatures, and fishes living among the rest, the balance of nature is in control, selecting only the weak to feed upon to survive!

The coyote friend, a cousin to wolf dog, lives to scavenge here in the meadow where the Nation's people hunt for food, taking only what they need, the rest to leave for another day. Winds contain currents to follow as a chill fills the air, gliding homeward-bound spirits, which live here where the Raven was born. Many of those spirits still control nights unknown, to conjure evil spirits that try to prevail over the local genteel. From civil rights to corruption galore, the lives of many find pain delivered by those in control ... in control or the past or present?

Here at this time, a man alone lives only for the offspring that he sired. These, contrary to the rule, believe in facts of life, not what people in control say for personal benefit and greed.

Nights fall softly on this small fishing town of destiny. Even to this day, more people come to stay. In a camp growing large, problems will arise more frequently. Thus, the Raven says love once profound here in this quaint little town has been waylaid by asking for more. Greed of the has overshadowed the truth of having enough, to having it all!

With troubled mind, the Raven journeys out over the sea looking to find a moment of tranquility. On this sunny day with beauty galore, the scent of death is found in waters below, put there by the corrupt Fat Money Bear.

Without food once found here galore, how will the people survive on this Nation's shore?

Flying back to land, Raven sees changes to this once pristine shoreline with sandbars trying to rebuild where man has made channels. Barrier Islands now contain homes, parks, hotels, and such. Setting down on the city's seawall, his mind ventures into the past, seeing and then comparing to now.

Back then was a struggling period of time for the Nation's people, accepting others from lands afar, sharing, teaching, as brother to brother, like the story told of Cain and Abel.

These people took what they wanted, then defied others to protest. They were simply in search of gold and other precious stone. Thinking to possess this metal made you great beyond reach and gave you control to have others do for you, to act without recourse.

Today the seawall has been extended out into the bay several times and yet there are those that wish to extend it more. One portion where the city extended sewer lines into the bay caused erosion, washing out underneath the southern portion. Here is when man blames nature or the environment instead of personal greed ... Fat Money Bear still searching for silver and gold.

While destruction is still taking place and people are moving in day after day, this once sleepy little fishing village is but an easement for the eyes. Where trawlers once lined the San Sebastian River, now stand pleasure craft of all types. In Matanzas Bay and Salt Run, these vessels for personal pleasure lay anchored.

Descendants of these first people who invaded this land, taking it away from the Nations who lived here first are now buying and selling to tourists, taking their gold and silver after many decades of the same, as their ancestors did.

Butterfly appears out of the blue, taking a personal look at this beautiful village, flying among cascades of flowers, grasses so green, and shrubbery galore, with carriages pulled by horses lining the bay front along the seawall.

Amazed, remarked Raven to Butterfly, while flying low and slow, "Here old things are where new things are built to be old again. The future is found by rebuilding the past so man can see how far he has come and not go there again!" Raven flies west looking down on a field named Francis where a grand hotel once stood and baseball was played back in the day, when kids would do such things and playing sports was done for pleasure, not as a thing you did for money. How shallow the well of life has become. With so many drinking from the cup of plenty, the water of life is running sort of low down here at the Fountain of Youth.

Suz loved the south where she finds the rays of sunshine, parrots, parakeets, and birds of all kinds speaking to her daily to bring her cheer. Up in the Dakotas, a white buffalo calf has been born. So is this to say that world peace is on the way? Or just another illusion playing with spirits that are trying to lead humanity in the wrong way, evil wonders that were conjured up to help mankind down in the swamps, to invade mystic lands of the Nations, and drain the land dry by planting sugarcane, controlling water by digging canals, and then the property sold by land speculators.

This day, humans see that what was done is harmful to nature and are trying to replace what was disturbed. As Raven glides silently across rivers of grass holding streams and lakes once abundant with life, now just dry land with sinkholes emerging in parts of the state swallowing homes, barns, and businesses built where creatures at one time lived before the population of humans began to "better control" nature's handmade estate, only to pursue the lure of Fat Money Bear to gather yellow gold on this money trail that some choose to follow.

Most times encompassing time involved trials and tribulations, working half of your life to be rich, the rest of your life spending your fortune to regain youth that you threw away making a fortune. The greatest fortune is to live without having to want for more than what satisfies you! Devotion to the direction that you wish to take comes through easement and peace of mind instilled through a chosen path that you follow to search and find your life!

As Raven follows these channels of current, seeing all within the context of the location at that time, and says not a word nor emits a warning sound, always romancing ideas, to reveal actions contained by mankind, to add, not detract from any thing's time here on earth.

There are whales in the sea, to tiny bumble bees, or microscopic organisms unseen by human eyes, there to keep humanity alive. The heat of love in humans, animals, and creatures produce, then produce again and again. This is the same for fishes, too. Here in this bowl of life, moment by moment feelings change and this soul-searching environment causing anticipation towards daily stagnation of life and worldly goods.

Dashing through torrents of seasonal rains emitted from clouds weeping in sorrow for their loss below is earth's gain so rivers may flow and grasses will grow with this moisture supplied by rain, Sam Raven swoops low across a farmer's potato field in which a potato bug hides, then crosses another farmer's cabbage field in which a cabbage worm is munching lazily on a leaf there in the sun.

Settling gently down on a nearby woods fence, the Raven watches quietly as humans prepare to spray insecticides over the crop to eradicate these so-called pests! Decreed by the Fat Money Bear, this special breed that considers money its honey of life and is always looking for a plump money hive to raid for more.

Butterflies, birds, and bees galore search out food and pollinate in return helping the farmers, too. The wonders of life are seldom seen and are different day to day. The stature of an animal's body is not the same externally. Inside, most are all the same. This operating system that runs a mammal's body works basically the same, with minute intricate differences controlled by the brain, sending messages to all systems of that creature's organism.

Ancient men such as Socrates and Plato, scholars both, would talk of things to come. Is that from mystic powers? Or just seeing the possibilities of things on the avenues of life that could be achieved? Why is it so hard to see the simple things in life created by a simple man or woman, as the case may be? To foretell a truth, without being ridiculed by others of the kind. Perhaps a human should take time to sit and watch the construction of a spider's web. With intricate care, time, and patience, a project is complete.

With the gust of a breeze, Raven lifts his wings and, with a few flaps, is in the air traveling away for another encounter someplace along the way.

Below, a church's spire beckons all to come. Here the anointed speak of better times to come after you are reborn again! Later, these same people lust for what they say is wrong in the sight of …

From times of ancient writings on a cave's wall, to ancient parchments or inscriptions in burial chambers when found, the power to believe in something or someone unseen tends to give power to a body and soul that in it believes! The goal of life, as seen by a child, is to grow to adult so life will be easier, to be able to do what you want to do, uncontrolled, after journeying into this realm of manhood or womanhood.

Fact is found, that to be able to live within a social society, a person must comply with the same rules and regulations that others do. To be accepted by fellow humans is the first goal, then to be able to aspire through mutual work is the second goal. The third goal is to be able to rise to a heaven above after death!

"Above what?" is a question found in the Blue Eyed Raven's head. After watching many nations bury their forms in many different ways, burned on funeral pyres, buried below the ground, encased in crypts of different sizes and shapes, always saying that they will rise another day into the sky. To travel far away and live in a great city with streets made of gold! I guess that city was built by the Fat Money Bear in a forest far away. Could humans survive without traveling down this hidden road towards a goal they set in their mind, and could this heaven above just be that a human's mind, the top most complex in body form, things that control everything in a body, and it is above?

Humans speak of rising above while looking up into the sky, or are they saying above while meaning returning into their own mind when they die?

As a child, they are born, and to which childhood do they return before they die? Then the children they begat will conceive and deliver a child that has similar traits to the one that has passed; thus, the saying *one shall never die, but live forever!*

The Raven ponders everyday life of every species here on earth, and in doing this, a common link is found. This common link is food. Causing things to grow, supports life; without it, things die slowly. Finding food sources today is getting harder for animals here on Mother Earth. Mankind kills for pleasure, not to survive; thereby, eradicating the food source for trophies to hang on the wall. Selling this wild meat and fish just adds to and makes larger the Fat Money Bear!

Raven's journey leads him down side roads of this village where he encounters six *brother* pigeons sitting in a row on a power line discussing actions of this day, comparing notes on the best area to feed and where the best berries are, and when they will ripen enough to eat.

Jessie pigeon says, "You know those squirrels are pretty slick. They try to get to the fruit first and take the best, then leave the ones too old for us." Not to interrupt, Raven just nods his head as he flies past on this day's off-road excursion down south. Along this road where a small creek used to flow stand homes and buildings. All the foliage has been cut away, leaving bare soil on an open plain. Two large "collecting ponds" were dug to retain water there, all for the Fat Money Bear. Even there, the trees and flowers are retained. A tear runs down the Raven's eye as he ventures on to view more future schemes of patrons to the Fat Money Bear.

Here families of beavers have built a large complex and work to improve it daily, working on it constantly to make it better, and in doing so, create avenues for others to benefit.

Solidly amused at all of this, Red Bird and the Crow call out in jest, passing ever so close to the drainage canal, knowing that it will surely flow into a river where food stuff live creating pollution that affects someone in some way sooner or later, don't you see?

This hurried lesson in nature and ecology comes from animals of nature that are being killed the same way mankind is killing himself - unknowingly, trying to create nourishment in *scientific* ways.

Back in the woods along a small creek, otters live and play eating daily. Will their food chain be affected through use of fertilizer and pesticide sprays?

Raven circles around to journey north to witness the invading of the serenity once held there in the swamps and woodland forests during times when a noted botanist traveled along its way, cataloguing, filing, naming unspecified flowers and foliage growing there for posterity!

How do you cut, clean, burn, and destroy in the name of progress, causing these animals, once so many, to be able to stay after taking their food and homes away? In their place there is a building - stone and steel structures -to take the place of trees and underbrush, then planting small areas to beautify the structures, but not for the animal's sake!

Chapter 9

Skimming over the cypress treetops, Raven sees a beautiful grassy lawn with ponds and fishes in the middle of nature; yet humans kill creatures that invade this protected land, creatures that search below the ground for food that they eat to stay alive, animals such as hogs or armadillos, then leave these animals to rot away or nature's beasts to consume them while the human plays on.

Once abundant in food for creatures galore, man marveled at so many, that he thought they would never be depleted. So in their haste with fire and advancement, trying to make things easy, man has shortened this path to destruction for many who wish to live a *fast life* in search of riches galore, when more is never enough.

Flying along the river that flows the wrong way, named St. Johns by explorers long ago, causes the Raven to pause atop a bald cypress tree as memories are recalled through the mind's instant replay, visions of natives crossing in wooden canoes or wading out to set or retrieve fish from traps while living on its banks. Weaving baskets made from material taken from the forest was a fast and easy way to carry things back to camp or to build a place to live that when you decided to leave, everything would be left the same as it was or you would just toss it into the fire used for cooking.

Today dark clouds were coming from the south with a smell of rain. Raven looking towards the east sees a small outline flying toward him. As time passes, the outline becomes clear to the eye. It's a lone pelican flying low, looking for a snug place to weather this storm. He lands on the docks along the shore to scavenge fish parts before the rain.

Raven wondered aloud where have all the pelicans gone? An answer followed: Down to the Keys! When people clean fish out on the dock, the pelicans quickly eat all of the parts. They don't save it or throw it into the waterways. The pelican spins around in flight, retreats from shore to water again, and after doing so, waves goodbye with a feather from behind.

Thoughts, aspirations, actions bring involvement in life's membership. Firewater brings out the real personality in men on journeys down, often dense cloud-covered trails, causing mishaps toward other beings instead of pulling toward a goal in life. A mind is filled with haze, making unsure steps on shaky ground, leaving foggy lives that can never be found. Alone, always searching for the thing they cannot find! Perhaps a ray of sunshine's sparkling beam will touch the crown of an ardent disbeliever in the heat of the day, bringing instant clarification to a clouded mind, giving reason, understanding, and love, instead of hurt, mistrust, and pain throughout this person's given days.

Unholy hours taken in jest are replaced with times of reflection so that positive things may be brought about in daily life, not daily strife, realizing where attitude has taken them and what they possess!

Unfulfilled dreams on roads never taken, or strolls along an avenue when thinking, it is too hard to do ... and never start saying that's easy to do, anybody can do that!

Taking the first step is always the hardest after trying. The realization is that it isn't so hard after all. Then a person has started their journey down a *different road* where others cannot go without washing dirt from their feet, as well as the feet of people that surround them, in humility and love. Washing is done by washing sins of the past from your hands, while cleaning wrongdoings from the past that were committed to the ones whose feet you wash.

Humility strengthens and cleanses a person's soul and instills power beyond control and strength beyond a mortal's dimension in times most needed! A love beheld by all of forgiving acts, to a humble word of thanks, and gentleness freely given to all; in these, help, praise, and understanding is given to all that need to be lifted up in times of distraught hurt, pain, and self-belief, while feeling the weight of the world upon their meager body's frame.

These simple things can be freely and openly given with a pure heart and an easy smile. Freely given, you shall freely receive! This Blue Eyed Raven tirelessly and constantly travels, as comments call and moments of wonder seem to aimlessly stall the realization beyond humanity's control when screams in the night are never heard. But the Raven sees and knows protection is provided by unseen powers beyond human control.

As the wind currents blow along the shore, many an updraft can come, as spirits in the night, catching unaware, but, Oh, what a delight, so easy to glide effortlessly, empowered to see far in advance; so high, all things earthward seem so small, and yet food can be seen readily available for birds of prey to scoop up and eat, just a long power dive, maybe skimming just above the water will cause surprise. Can you imagine being lifted into the air without your being aware?

Time so flies ... or time sure flies, repeated stanzas of melancholy verse heard over waves across this earth. Another verse often shouted is time sure flies when you're having fun! Waves of sound carried through space from place to place, non-visible to the naked eye, traveling at a speed only a mathematician can comprehend. No longer bound to stately earth, man has started to understand that observing creatures placed here to share will offer more to humanity than sustenance to survive.

With the coming of age, humanity seems to suggest knowledge, but proclaims stupidity as wealth.

The Raven's journey is far from complete, as again he lifts his large wings against a breeze and instantly takes flight. With one mighty flap, over the countryside he soars, flying over ice frozen since time began at the top and bottom poles. Both the North Pole and the South Pole, animals living here are thick-coated with fur and fat, their bodies designed to live here, where life separates omnivorous men of humanity's clan.

Observing life here is no more or no less hectic, just placed in a different location, time, and space, forever cognizant of beings feeding on other beings. For sustaining life here, in this defining world where there isn't place for mistakes, two factors are omnipresent there between slow or quick: It is either alive or dead. There is no in between. A creature wounded will be claimed by a beast or the environment.

Man is not built to survive in this climate without special clothing and homes. Food to eat and constant monitoring from the lower 48 is mandatory, just in case something goes wrong or a person has to be replaced.

Here the fowl do not fly. Only when the weather gets warmer do birds fly close to the cold area, but not close enough that it will endanger their lives. Then they fly closer to a warmer zone when winter comes. Birds that live where it is cold are called penguins. This flightless bird also lives, hunts, and plays in water of the sea. Clumsy looking on land as they waddle around, these birds is dominant, quick, and beautiful to watch in the water.

These flightless birds, when in the sea, represent the finest of fisherman. Animals such as these only take what is needed to survive, never killing for sport like orcas, or as they are known, *killer whales*; which sometimes, in their hunt, will get a seal, begin throwing it into the air until it tires and cannot escape, then bites it in two and swallows the meat.

Is this a pattern or just a way of acting out unknown behavior? The Blue Eyed Raven sees many things to ponder!

On a blast of Nordic air, again he lifts his wings and takes to the air for a jaunt to Siberia to watch some yak-taming by natives living there. This local animal was tamed to be a beast of burden, to pull sleighs loaded with things that make it possible for people to survive by having transportation, while also giving milk to drink and meat to eat. This animal is a mainstay to these Siberian nomadic people.

Sheep and goats are to desert wanderers as the camel is to Arabs. Each civilization in different parts of the earth all have ways to survive or different foods to eat. A base was formed with different types of plants, animals, and locations given to each group of humans when they were told "With these things that have been provided for you, you must find out how to use them for your survival!"

When some are used in the wrong way or in excess, they will cause discomfort or death; while some in the same respect will counteract the first, making you well again!

Animals know which things to eat to help them grow or things to eat that will keep them alive. Humanity observed this sort of thing and to this point has grown without the help of native animals to sustain the lives of humans, or how would they have remained alive to reproduce and become the dominant one?

Only traces of time shall be the one to explain this rule. In future periods of time, searching *for a new direction* contained in this vast universe that we today have the pleasure to live within!

Chapter 10

Back into a swirl of wind, Raven finds warmth in the sun's rays gathering around his body and playing frolic across his wings, while in slow motion, dances over his head, down his back, and rolls leisurely off of his tail, giving a smack of energy to his forlorn feathers, which are stationary in his "after guidance system," more generally known as *The Tail.*

A gracious feeling comes over the Raven, as the earthly greatness unfolds below. Unspoiled views, only changed by a stroke of the brush held in the painter's mystical hand of nature!

Knowing few see what is offered by the wearing blinders every day, so their direction never changes and they will not lose their way ... Behold a bird that wings its way to a destination abroad, then returns the same way, never failing to know the course. Humanity, I'm afraid, does not qualify!

After leaving the traveled track, they break away, trying to set their own pace to make their own way, cutting a new road or path. Rising each heavenly morn, giving thanks for another beautiful day or rising in that same morning only to be down-hearted and forlorn, thinking *What is there for me to do today,* instead of thanking someone for giving you great expectations to brighten your way.

When Raven swoops through giant pillars of stone counting rooms for humans in which to live, he calls to memory the rock dwellers, a small fury animal living here for safety's sake. How then does this compare and what is the difference it makes?

People of the Nation's live within the boundaries of nature, trying to be humble enough to stay, asking to only share food and water with all earth's creatures so all will live and be aware to save enough for another day! These people of the Nations are not different, just humanity thinks of *priorities* in different ways. There isn't a demand for silver or gold, only that each band of people be left alone to hunt, fish, live where they please without having to pay for land that their *Great Spirit* owns and belongs to no one, but is free for all to use and not destroy.

Nature controls this Mother Earth. No more or less, all things move in a rhythm with life. To change this beat causes destruction for man and, in doing so, causes destruction for life all around! Is it so far-fetched to have a goal to reach, and without a goal in sight, would you attempt anything?

People are asked why they climb a mountain? *To reach the top*! Is an answer given. Why isn't the answer *To be first*! Humans need to make their mark to be recognized during their lifetime, and in doing so, are raised up by their peers for self-satisfaction and gratification.

The Raven is always aware of a sense given to man: one of hostility, greed, and power, as one feeds off of the other. Like an animal that consumes others to grow bigger and stronger, and can only be killed by a bigger animal of the same breed.

Raven's feathers hold the secret that, in time, will tell of things for humanity's peace, because though this Nation's door opened slightly at first, then opened wide for the cascade of all to come flooding in, only to bring sin, corruption, pestilence, and plague, trying to kill off the humble and good for humanity's sake.

Or is the human today just misunderstood? Moving to areas where plenty is at hand, taking until there is but few to none left, then moving away, leaving all of his destruction behind for others to clean up and then start all over again. In some areas, the residue of *stuff* buried underground has caused problems today and the future ahead. What path will be taken before all are dead?

Winter's swirl comes suddenly, causing the Raven to turn south toward the equator again to gather fruits, nuts, and berries brought forth at this seasonal period of time, to frolic with friends in tree canopies and observe life today compared to times of the past when that was the regional hub for humanity in the Americas, the continent of that day! Back then, there were simple people of native towns where all were content to live life that they knew just quietly day by day, alone but together when trouble arose, to harness nature's plenty, to raise crops to eat, when distant thunder brought men of a different shore to conquer for riches and gold, doing this in the name of their god who died to save mankind's soul?

Feelings of the heart often unseen are focused through actions subtle at first, then raised to a higher degree when noticed by another one of the opposite sex. Through the mystery of mind, sometimes mistakes take place and the same types are attracted to each other, but cannot reproduce.

The Raven was astonished through times of this practice taking place, and found that the mostly gentle were the ones that practiced it. In the animal world, the macaw with a few others, can talk or make sounds like humans of the day. Is this a mistake, or can all species communicate through a telepathic wavelength that has no bounds? The Raven says, "As I believe, I shall say!"

Humans of today are trying to advance through studies of animal sounds and their mind wavelengths trying to find a way to communicate to them so they may use them in war, and if they are killed, a human is saved. This practice by humans seems to be taking them in reverse, killing each other and animals, thinking that they are progressing to who knows where? So believe in life after death or reincarnation.

A story told was that what if you don't believe in, and died, then found out there was no heaven? Or what if you believed in, and died, and found out there was? Humans in the past have found that to bring people together to accomplish goals, they must have something or someone that leads in a way to give them inner strength for doing what must be done, to give direction to their personal life in times of desolation as well as happiness.

Strength of mind enables strength of body and soul to overcome daily strife, as well as confliction with mental waves of thought radiating from the past, future, and beyond!

Inner beings belong to the space of time, only to live in a given form for a certain length of time. Then that space is vacated until another space is made available, at which time that spirit lingers in limbo waiting, always waiting for the right time and place ... or just another day.

A *spirit* yells out, if only the Raven knew what, "*Just give me a chance to be born over again!*"

A human is seen growing to be adult. In these formative years is when they are tried. Either they will become worthy of life or be cast back into the furnace fires to be recast again. The ones without merit will have their mold broken and thrown away so no reproduction will ever be made!

As the Raven follows the dreams provided by nature's innermost schemes, taking of actions throughout history deems pertinent again after reading of these episodes later in history, a magazine entitled *Archeology*. These scientific methods provide information gathered, telling where and how those early arrivals ate, quartered, and built wells to draw fresh water so life could be more easily lived.

Never does it retell personal thoughts in someone's day, tales they told or apprehensions contained in everyday life of these mortal men and women, trying to find a more pleasant sort of life without rules placed upon them by monarch's dictators in lands ruled by this sort.

Humanity has searched for freedom to live in as well as to live for freedom, no matter how long or brief it may be. In actions, let not your good be evil spoken of. This, in doing, refers to help given to a neighbor as you would expect someone to provide help to you, if the same action befell upon you at some given time of your life here on earth. Again, the Bible, humanity's guidebook to perfect reasoning states *Neither a borrower or lender be*, suggesting to mortals that it is easier to live without peeling a wandering eye towards what another might have, but to work diligently towards daily tasks that will provide all of these things that you wish to have after you complete labor and maintain a pure heart; all the while side-stepping obstacles cast down to create stumbling blocks along your path of life traversed in this Garden of Eden placed forth for mankind to use and live in without sin or misrepresenting truth.

For insomuch as doing one thing wrong, the mortals have broken their vow; at which time, they will be cast out of this place of peace to live in constant turmoil enslaved upon them through their actions towards other mortal men. In doing so, humanity has no one to blame for hardships except themselves and actions taken towards other mortal men.

Females, on the other hand, are different in ways of accomplishing goals, while arriving at or achieving same effect towards the end of given goal.

Raven's observation tells of such things taken from tales past long since, handed down from tribes in Indian camps.

Story is told of two brothers bold, traveling through life's hardened trail, both wishing to be more than the other could be. As children growing tall, one would do something, then the other compelled to achieve a greater task: Tit for Tat. You do this and I'll do that. Trying to better each other's action.

Then came the day when a beautiful maiden passed their way. Without delay, each one tried to win her favor through feats that other mortals where unable to come close to achieving in hopes of impressing her enough that she would choose one to be her companion for life. In the end of this story, it's told that these two brothers so bold, married not, and throughout time grew stronger and more bold to earn them the given names of Hate and Deceit! As for the maiden both pursued, she married and gave birth to two named Honesty and Truth!

Time has no way of telling which one does provide or which one will not. Daily action and knowledge separates runners into different categories when entering life's race of approval competition considered utmost in human's society.

The Raven defies actions believed to be different in some, when each one is the same, containing all parts the same. The action learned means future told, accomplishing things better, rather than for only! Individuals are one entity in one body containing how many souls?

This thing called a brain is so complex that use of all would be unknown, the power it could hold and how it would be used is what humanity tries to decipher. Does the saying *less means more* or *more means less*? Use of the same holds clues to life's fulfillment or demise contained in this stature of man. Held tightly, wrapped in threads of a delicate weave, the strength of which is never seen, only to gather in strife, turmoil, in relief given, held tightly by this thing called love!

This has been directed in history past, given to mortals in time. Always being related to or appearing in the same movement of life from beginning of time to present. Just look around at the people living, acting, being in love, through emotions, places, things depicted in degrees of which is controlled by a human's brain center control.

The Raven taps the well of wealth and renown during a testing period in writing his first book in time, withstanding personal ridicule of masters in compiled verses, thought so quaint in speech and rhyme, voicing thoughts to be placed in a fellow's mouth so that, when spoken, they just roll off the given tip of tongue. It's filling space of air, void with gentle, soothing musical sound, of which flows so lightly across and through a fresh spring afternoon, air filling ears with various sensations of thrill and excitement, that so rapidly falls directly downward to become rested upon the gentle maiden's virginal strings wound around her heart to be plunked and strummed tenderly by this stranger dancing through nightly dreams so vividly ... so clear.

Alas, these thoughts so clear may never be shared, only with a close friend, one so dear that to the grave these secrets will accompany. This friend, one so dear, that thoughts are shared together. Thinking back in time when we were so close as a little ones, then with age, growth, change of inner feelings, while walking beside of a once-trickling stream has now become a raging torrent inside of a mote, encircling a sturdily-built fortress that holds the Raven's heart of mine.

Admitting only a chosen few to cross the bridge of love that will draw shut at the sign of attack, keeping all from breaking this fragile heart held so pure, intact with thought of giving only to that special one that will win true love contained inside of the Raven. To him, she will be true, and to no other will be given her love held for the one and only one who is made especially for her. Sharing only private moments with that one, so when the deepest memories are made to be in place for everlasting days upon days in memory's files, to be drawn out of secret places within *your* mind.

Making memories are special to some; others remember, but cannot retrieve those feelings had at that personal time when seconds became endless.

With your mind in celestial bliss, flowers everywhere, smelling so sweet, the music you hear flows so gently across and through channels of your mind, creating strong muscular hands, caressing parts of your body that you have never felt could be feeling so great. From the crown of your head to tips of your toes, a rolling, rippling effect starts. Then, as it moves downward, becomes so intense that it feels as if you're going to explode and disappear to never be seen again, wishing, moving, trying to cry out, calling for help, mercy, relief, anything.

Then within less than a blink of an eye, total relief, *celestial feeling of peace*, pleasure, and aim returns to the body from which it has been entrapped. This mortal frame that searched for just the right one. In finding love for the first time, reasoning is cast aside, finding pleasure-only-seeking of men!

While the female is trying to be enthroned into the class known as motherhood, fulfilling her role here on earth to perpetuate the human species, given to at this special place in time down here on *Mother Earth*!

Flashing fields of bountiful biscuits laden with flowing rivulets running over in honey and jam, a steaming platter of fresh cooked ham smoked inside of small house built for nothing more than that particular purpose, smoking seasonal hams, fish, or wild meat killed during times of the hunt, flashes of dreams brought forward in this timely art of thought *good as it may seem* doesn't fill an empty place in the bodies of men. A space taken from a book of settler's known to fill an empty stomach, work must first be done, then all will be made possible by sweat of the brow, taken from people working through use of their hands directed by a clean and civil mind.

Chapter 11

Raven yearns for days when solitude and peace will return to places given for man to maintain, and not destroy, as keepers of this earthly ground. Through a vision last night, Raven saw Mary Anne, a maiden who played an earnest part in Raven's feelings.

Once, near death, she came to Raven with her mother by her side telling Raven to live again, and then she went away. Two times through many moons, I thought that I saw her, but maybe not. Like a dream, she would appear to let me know she was near. Then as if in a dream, she would disappear, then unexpectedly reappear at some place, some time, some year.

To Maiden Mary Anne, I bequeath wealth and happiness to fulfill her throughout her years. Ahem, alas, my stories but run cold this eve as memories past brighten fires of stories told growing further into the dimness of worldly woe.

This fire of faith, with kindling aglow, shall be fed through night times to frighten away wandering spirits traversing round people's doors. Tales of death, destruction, and woe tell no tales before this light of campfire so bright. Never can be death, destruction, and woe be welcomed by people speaking the truth. To this world so easily led by flowers of gold, realizing never too late that they were papier-mâché, placed there to sway thoughts in people searching for the magic metal called gold.

That stuff that will change men's soul, never meaning to corrupt, only after finding that magic stuff will cause a person to kill to have that and more. To enlighten this darkened world, brightness of gold brings forth fires of delight, burning day and night. Being rich for a while lasts as long as a gold vein flows, causing crippling of men searching for the hidden mother lode someplace below ground, somewhere on this earthly world.

The Raven's mind will take another track in thinking this day. Humanity is starting to think of ways to preserve the ecology on earth, forlorn as it may seem. Advancement in recycling water has become a topmost issue of the day. Concerned citizens of humanity speak out concerning lackadaisical use of this much-needed liquid found in underground aquifers used to sustain said water supply.

Today, knowledge learned should be knowledge given for enlightenment of humanity's growing species of mankind. Total acceptance is farfetched at this time, with mortals seeking ways to supply this needed potion for retention of humankind here on this earthly home.

Could this need be replaced in thought, as water retention being the preverbal mother lode in riches that mortals search for, endlessly seeking below ground, not yellow in color, but a clear liquid that is far more valuable when there is less then what humanity needs?

Travel, therefore, in ways and days enhanced through thought, thinking how society of this day may suffer as well as act to rationing of water for drinking purposes, only not to mention strategic use in work-related use.

Negative options arise, yet in this day towards consumption, use in a mountain's water supply, far into heights, soaring sky-high, collecting moisture carried in clouds, then letting it fall onto the parched earth below, beginning first earthly voyage, seeping below ground level to find channels of the same, then drifting on down lazily together, finding rivers hidden far below contentedly rushing headlong into the sea from which this droplet of fallen rain will again be lifted into the heavens to ride within a cloud, gathering moisture, until it will become too heavy, and then it will return to earth for yet another journey, bringing life to nature's own. All because of this simple drop of rain! Its journey not too often intensely catalogued, just taken for granted that it will always be there and will never fail in providing nature's own life-giving rain!

Humans today are constantly reminded to conserve while actively using their time here on earth. Do you suppose that it really will sink in to the dense matter called a brain to benefit others on down life's dust-covered, rocky trail that may be called one day a road?

Blue eyes peering into darkness of thought, searching memory banks, passing from now into eons of space, inserting into a void filled with spirits, past yet positively bold expressing waves containing thought within beams of sunlight, mortal men will behave differently living in sunbeams instead of a damp, dark cave! Emotions vary as they may remain a constant level in sunlight or a dark cave.

Reorganization is a positive for animals of all species, type and kind. Remarkably, the Raven sees two that have parted from *one in marriage* to *two separate souls* trying to find out what is for them on the other side, things forbidden, times before are now common to please. Once belonging to one another was the only thing that pleased, and now friends past are again friends indeed, expressing feelings held back in younger days flow easily to people that are close as friends.

Chapter 12

Flying easily along the ocean's coast, the Raven takes note of articles found lying among cast-away periods of time, things as simple as driftwood that at one time held great handmade sails used to transport vessels across the water to fish, trade, or just venture out for reasons of their own.

Placing fear, fact, and reasoning to the forefront of emotions during traversing courses unknown without knowledge obtained from journey-men before, the Raven offers a thought today: That throughout history, someone traveled afar and returned to tell of these things they encountered so others may go later in time.

Communication was not as available then as it is in modem days. This, to the Raven, is why advancement was slow for humanity in the early days of yore. Thinking of how humans felt when deciding the use of the wheel would be easy for travel and to carry goods, do you think humans made articles to transport by hand before a lazy person found use of the wheel? Maybe an injured person needed help or a person who just thought ahead of their time developed the wheel. Did it originate in one place, was observed by a foreign traveler, and idea was taken afar to be used in another's world?

This would be how things were made better to use when the same type of material was not available in that region. Whatever is developed, someone someplace will try to enhance it in a more functional way to make it better, then profit from someone's original idea!

The Raven sees ancient valuables being washed ashore from decades past from ships of conquering nations, transporting captured goods of war. These same articles found today are much more valuable to some in humanity who dare to live for travels on the trail of gold leading to other nations.

Other things visible to the naked eye are forms of fish that have died and washed ashore. There are undocumented species today that man has never seen, creatures that live so far below the surface of oceans blue, where humans have not been able to go before.

In the early days, these creatures, when seen, caused a fright to humanity who in response created tales of lore of monsters coming from the deep, attacking ships, and devouring all. Later, with advancement through the ages, these creatures are no longer feared, just found to be animals that live here on earth and are not readily seen by humans.

Fishing these waters blue are turtles, sea birds, crustaceans galore, with humans casting nets from boats or wading near shore, looking to catch a big fish, one that would cause murmurs to roar as to how great this feat was and how only a man who was a great fisherman could do this, thus adding height to the stature to one of that community. People would say then, "There goes the one who caught that big fish. Don't you know that was a thrill?"

And did you ever think about the fish? Fishing for food is necessary. Fishing for fun is not. Catching and bragging rights are claimed, after which the thrill is gone!

Memories are things left to abide, keeping you attuned to what you have done, immersed in tranquil thoughts that bring back a story told of fishing on the beach.

Made in the USA
Las Vegas, NV
09 November 2021

34068981R00049